Ice

Leighann Dobbs

This is a work of fiction.

None of it is real. All names, places, and events are products of the author's imagination. Any resemblance to real names, places, or events are purely coincidental, and should not be construed as being real.

She glanced at her watch, her stomach twisting when she realized they were ten minutes late in serving the ice cream. The event had been planned down to the minute with various family members making speeches and presentations at set times. The big finale was supposed to come after dessert when Regis Banks himself would address the guests, giving his thanks and making a much anticipated announcement.

Lexy noticed Regis' personal secretary, Cora, standing watch in the dark shadows of the corner of the room, a scowl aimed in Lexy's direction. Cora's mouth was pursed in a tight line, her dark eyes shooting daggers. Cora had planned the event with Anna and Lexy, stressing over and over that the timing was critical. But surely, a mere ten minutes wouldn't be that much of a problem?

"Better get a move on," Anna whispered, jerking her chin in Cora's direction.

Lexy nodded and took a deep breath before she started across the wide pine flooring to the head table.

As she passed the round guest tables, she noticed the busboys had cleared the dinner plates. The guests were sipping from their coffee cups and eyeing the desert trays expectantly as a photographer made the rounds taking candid shots.

Lexy started at one end of the head table. Making sure to take the ice cream dishes from the tray in the right order, she set them down in front of the guests one by one, taking care that her slightly shaking hands didn't spill any sauce on the tablecloths.

She could feel Cora's gaze boring into her back and she served as quickly as she could, then ran back to the kitchen for the next tray.

Two more trips back to the kitchen and Lexy and Anna had finished serving all the tables. At the last table, Lexy's grandmother, Mona Baker, or Nans as Lexy called her, was seated with her friends Ruth, Ida and Helen. Lexy didn't know how, but somehow Nans had finagled an invitation to the posh affair and the four ladies sat giggling like schoolgirls as they dipped spoons into their ice cream.

Lexy stood behind them attempting to blend into the background, like any good caterer would.

"These madeleines are divine, Lexy. You wouldn't happen to have any extra, would you?" Ruth half-turned in her seat to look at Lexy.

"I might have some," Lexy said. "I'll run to the kitchen after Regis' speech starts and bring some over."

"Shhh!" Ida put her hand on Ruth's arm. "He's standing up."

All eyes turned to the head table where Regis Banks pushed his way up from his chair.

"He's still pretty spry for one-hundred," Helen said.

"Yeah, he's a looker, too," Nans replied.

"And rich," Ida jabbed Helen in the ribs. "Maybe you should make a move on him."

"Oh, stop it!" Helen sputtered, her face turning red.

Lexy watched as Regis straightened his tie and cleared his throat. He *did* look pretty spry for his age. He stood with ease, not bent over like one might expect. Lexy noticed he didn't even use a cane. And he looked pretty good, too. Tall and thin with a full head of thick white hair.

Lexy had heard he was sharp as a tack and still took a daily interest in the business he'd built from scratch. She also heard he ruled with an iron fist and kept a miserly control over the family money. That's probably why he was a multimillionaire.

"I'd like to thank everyone for attending my birthday," Regis started and then waited as the room broke into applause. He had a strong and steady voice. Lexy found it hard to believe the guy was a century old.

"And I especially would like to thank my loving family for arranging this great party," Regis continued.

As Regis droned on, Lexy studied the head table. To Regis' left sat his oldest son, Winston. Lexy guessed that Winston was in his late sixties. He looked stuffy in a starched white collar with blue suit and tie. A redhead, still attractive even in her mid-sixties, sat stiffly next to him—probably his wife. From the way they were sitting, Lexy could tell they weren't getting along.

On the other side of the wife sat Regis' other son, Lawrence. From what Lexy had heard, Lawrence was the odd man out in the family. Where Regis and Winston were interested in business and money, Lawrence was more of a tree-hugger with no head for business. He preferred more leisurely activities and was known to be into conservation and ecology. Where Regis and Winston were stuffed shirts, Lawrence was laid back. This was evidenced by his tie, which resembled the print on a Hawaiian shirt.

Lawrence wasn't paying much attention to Regis. Instead he had his head bent toward a man in his early forties that sat next to him—a grandchild, Lexy figured. There were several people in their thirties and forties at the table and she assumed them to be Regis' grandchildren.

On the right side of Regis sat his daughter, Olivia. Olivia looked a lot younger than her brothers—maybe early to mid-fifties, although her youthful appearance might have had some help surgically. Lexy didn't know any of the Banks very well, but the rumors of Olivia having a penchant for expensive fashion must have been true judging by her dazzling couture dress, Kate Spade purse and Jimmy Choo stilettos.

On the other side of Olivia sat two couples in their forties—more grandchildren, Lexy supposed. Cora hovered unobtrusively in the background behind Regis.

Ruth caught Lexy's eye and looked pointedly at the madeleine. Regis was still droning on.

Now would be the perfect time to grab the extra madeleines from the kitchen, Lexy thought, heading in the direction of the stainless steel doors.

Lexy scanned the tables as she crossed the room to see if anyone needed a coffee refill. She was almost to the kitchen door when a strangled sound jerked her attention toward the head table.

Regis Banks let out a strangled cough, then loosened his shirt collar and continued in a raspy voice. "And now, I'd like to announce—"

He stopped abruptly, clawing at his neck. He made a sickening gurgling sound then slumped into his chair, his eyes rolling back in their sockets right before his head fell forward, face first, into his bowl of ice cream.

Chapter Two

The room fell silent for a few seconds while everyone stared at Regis' still body.

Then it erupted in action.

Winston shot out of his seat, the chair clattering to the ground behind him.

"Dad!" He pulled Regis' head out of the bowl, pressing his fingers to the older man's neck.

"Daddy!" Olivia squealed from Regis' other side.

Lawrence stood up, worry etched on his face, and helped Winston lay Regis out on the floor.

Nans dug her cell phone out of her purse and called nine-one-one while they performed CPR.

"Get out of the way. I'm a doctor." A man stood up from one of the tables and made his way to the head table. Lexy couldn't really see what was going on from where she stood—they had laid Regis down on the other side of the table, which blocked her view.

Her heart raced as she watched the crowd gathering around the old man's body.

The doctor pushed his way to the middle, then knelt down. A few seconds later, he stood, placing his hand on Winston's shoulder, which was still bobbing up and down as he performed chest compressions.

"It's no use," the doctor said gently. "He's gone."

Lexy gasped along with the rest of the crowd. She turned back to look at Nans, Ruth, Ida and Helen, but the ladies seemed to be taking it in stride. Anna, on the other hand, was not as calm. She stood behind Nans' table wringing a white cloth kitchen towel in her hands, her face drained of color.

Lexy rushed to her side. "Are you all right?"

"I don't know. I've never had a client die on me before."

Lexy pushed Anna into a chair next to Nans who took her hand, patting it soothingly. Ida pushed her untouched whiskey sour toward Anna.

"Drink up, this will help calm you," Ida said.

Anna obeyed, gulping the drink and then practically spitting it out.

"It's not like it should be a surprise to anyone that Regis Banks would die," Helen said amidst Anna's choking noises. "I mean he *was* one-hundred years old."

Ruth nodded. "He had a good long life."

"Guess you missed your chance," Ida said to Helen, a mischievous glint in her eye.

"Ida! That's inappropriate!" Helen hissed.

14

Nans had been unusually quiet all this time, her eye on the front of the room where the EMT's had arrived and were looking over the body. "I wonder why they aren't removing the body ..."

Lexy's head swiveled toward the front. "What do you mean? They're probably just doing ... whatever it is that they do. It takes time to go through their procedure, doesn't' it?"

"Not usually this much time. I mean, once there's nothing they can do, they usually just cart the body off," Nans said. "Unless ..."

Lexy frowned at her grandmother. "Unless what?"

The four older women exchanged raised eyebrow looks and a feeling of unease started to bloom in Lexy's stomach. Her grandmother and friends had a strange hobby—they investigated murders. It was more than a hobby, actually. They'd even had business cards printed with their name—*The Ladies Detective Club.*

Lexy had to admit, they did have a good record on solving cases and they'd even helped out the police on occasion. The problem was they sometimes saw murder where there was none ... and the death of Regis Banks surely wasn't murder.

"Oh, come on," Lexy said. "You guys must be bored because you haven't had a case lately. Regis wasn't murdered here in front of everyone. He was one-hundred years old. You saw yourself, his heart just gave out. It's certainly understandable at his age."

"Well, of course it *would* be, my dear." Ruth said, her eyes on the door. "But if that's the case, then what is our favorite homicide detective doing here?"

***

Lexy whipped her head toward the door. Ruth was right. Lexy's husband, homicide detective Jack Perillo and his partner John Darling were standing there talking to the EMT's.

Across the table, Anna's china blue eyes were wide with alarm. "Homicide?"

"What?" Lexy's brows mashed together. "That's crazy. I'm going to ask Jack."

She stood, catching Jack's eye. He held up his finger, indicating that he'd be over when he finished with the EMT's. Lexy sat back down.

"Let's make a list of suspects." Ruth grabbed her beige patent leather old-lady purse from the back of her chair and rummaged inside, pulling out an iPad which she placed on the table in front of her.

"I know his wife is long dead, but did he have a girlfriend?" Nans asked.

"I bet he did. A young one," Ida offered. "I bet he wrote her into the will and she killed him off for the money."

The others nodded their agreement. Ruth tapped a note into the iPad.

"Wait a minute." Lexy held up her hand. "This is some kind of mistake. I'm sure Jack is here for some other reason."

"Some reason other than what?" Jack asked, appearing at Lexy's side.

"Other than murder," she answered, looking up into his honey-brown eyes. "Please tell us that's *not* why you're here."

Jack slid his eyes toward the front of the room. "Well, I can't tell you if Mr. Banks was *murdered,* but we were called because his death might be suspicious."

"Really?" Ida's eyes twinkled.

"I knew it!" Ruth exclaimed.

Anna sucked down the rest of the whiskey sour and grabbed the fruity umbrella drink from the table in front of Ruth.

"Suspicious, how?" Lexy asked.

"Mr. Banks didn't die of natural causes," Jack said.

"What? We all saw him die. It looked like a heart attack to me," Lexy said.

Jack nodded. "It probably did. But the EMT's noticed evidence that he died from anaphylaxis."

"What's that?" Anna asked as she noisily slurped the drink through the straw.

"An allergic reaction," Nans said. "Can cause swelling, hives, vomiting, low blood pressure…"

"My cousin is allergic to bees. She has to carry an epi-pen in case she gets stung. She has to inject herself right away or she could die." Anna turned her big blue eyes, which Lexy noticed were starting to become slightly unfocused, on Jack. "Is that what happened to Mr. Banks?"

Jack nodded. "His throat swelled, making it impossible to breathe."

Lexy cringed. "How awful. But I don't remember seeing any bees in here."

Jack's eyes darkened as he looked back up to the head table. She followed his gaze to where John was putting Regis' ice cream bowl into a large plastic bag. John sealed the bag, then turned and walked toward them at the back of the room.

"Hi, Lexy," John pushed his long ponytail back over his shoulder as he greeted her.

"Hi, John." Lexy eyed the plastic bag in his hand.

"I see you are in the middle of a controversy once again," he teased.

Lexy laughed. She didn't mind being teased by John. They were good friends as he was not only her husband's partner, he was also married to her best friend and assistant at her bakery *The Cup and Cake*.

The truth was, she *did* have a knack for ending up in the middle of a crime. It had happened several times—in fact, she'd met Jack when she'd been accused of killing her ex-fiance. But this wasn't a crime ... was it?

"What's with the bag? I thought you would be looking for a bee," Lexy asked, her stomach already sinking at the look on John's and Jack's faces.

"It isn't only bee stings that cause anaphylaxis. Food allergies can cause it, too." Jack looked pointedly at the ice cream.

"Food allergies? You mean like peanut butter?" Anna wavered in her chair. "We served peanut butter sauce on the ice cream, but some of the Banks family were allergic to peanuts. That's why we had to be extra careful when serving them."

All eyes turned to Lexy and she felt her stomach sinking. *She'd* served the ice cream to the head table. But she was sure she'd been very careful to give the bowls to the appropriate persons.

"Yes, exactly like peanut butter." Jack's eyes slid to the plastic bag then back to Lexy. "Is there any way you might have served peanut butter sauce to Regis Banks?"

Lexy shook her head. "No, I'm sure I set the tray up properly and served in the right order."

She had, hadn't she?

She had been kind of rushed but Lexy took food serving very seriously. She was certain she hadn't screwed up.

John shrugged. "Well it could have been an accident. Maybe he switched spoons with someone or tasted someone else's dish."

"Right," Lexy said hollowly. "It must have been an accident."

Anna gave Lexy a woeful look and Lexy's heart twisted. "I'm sure it was an accident. A horrible accident. But that can't be good for business … for either of us."

Chapter Three

"Accident my patootie." Nans handed Lexy the now clean, metal ice cream container which was the last of the catering equipment they were packing into the back of Anna's van.

"You don't really think someone gave him the peanut sauce on purpose, do you?" Lexy asked. "I mean, they seemed like a close family."

"*Seemed* like," Nans replied. "On the surface it looked that way, but anyone could see there was conflict going on underneath."

Lexy screwed up her face. She hadn't noticed any conflict. "I think you're just looking for an excuse to investigate something."

"No. I'm sure something funny is going on," Nans said. "I know you would never screw up something as important as that, especially when there's a food allergy involved."

"I hope not," Anna glanced nervously at the van. "I just bought this van and the bad publicity could kill my business."

Lexy's heart crunched at the worry on Anna's face. What if she *had* screwed up? "Don't worry, Anna. None of this was your fault. If I accidentally served him the peanut sauce, I'll own up to it and make sure it doesn't hurt your business."

"It won't come to that, right girls?" Ruth looked from Nans to Ida to Helen who all nodded their agreement.

"That's right," Ida added as she stuffed a folded napkin bulging with the left-over madeleines into her large purse. "You girls have nothing to worry about— *The Ladies Detective Club* is on the case!"

Helen patted Lexy's arm. "Don't worry, Lexy, we'll get to the bottom of it."

Lexy smiled at the four older women, her heart warming. It was nice to have friends that stuck by you even if it might turn out that she did make a mistake. But she felt certain she hadn't.

She tucked the ladies into Ruth's gigantic blue Oldsmobile and watched them drive off, wincing when Ruth took the turn too wide, running over a patch of white petunias that had been planted on the corner.

Lexy turned back to Anna who was climbing into the catering van. "Don't worry, Anna. Everything will be okay."

Anna gave her a wan smile. "I know. I just wish Mr. Banks hadn't died in the middle of the party."

"Or while eating my ice cream," Lexy added. "I'll call you later when I find out what Jack has to say."

"Thanks." Anna smiled, put the van in gear and drove off, leaving Lexy alone in the parking lot with her yellow VW bug.

Lexy took the long way home to give herself time to think. It was possible someone had switched the ice cream dishes. But who would want to kill Regis? And who would have been able to do that without anyone noticing?

She tried to think back to who had visited the head table, but she'd been pretty busy serving and hadn't had her eye on it the whole time. She knew there was a lot of milling about—almost everyone at the party went up to the table to congratulate Regis after dinner.

Which meant that almost everyone at the party was a possible suspect.

Lexy tried to clear her head as she turned into her neighborhood. Nans must be rubbing off on her. Now *she* was looking at everything with a suspicious mind. Most likely, it was just an accident. She'd know more once she talked to Jack.

A tinge of nervousness ran through her as she thought of Jack. He wasn't happy about the way she always seemed to get herself mixed up in the middle of murder cases. She hoped he wouldn't be mad at her.

Lexy pulled into the driveway of the 1940s bungalow she shared with Jack. The house had been Nans and when Nans had moved into the local retirement community, she'd sold it to Lexy. Now that Lexy and Jack were married, he'd moved in and they were preparing Jack's house for sale.

Lexy opened the front door and was immediately assaulted by a flurry of white fur. Her Shih-Tzu Poodle mix, Sprinkles, leaped at her knees in her usual over-exuberant greeting. She bent down to scoop the little dog into her arms.

"You're home." Jack made his way to her with a glass of wine. Taking the dog from her arms, he kissed her, then shoved the wine into her hand. "I thought you could use this."

Lexy smiled, feeling a little relieved. He wasn't mad.

"Thanks." She accepted the drink, kicked her shoes off and collapsed on the couch. It had been a long day and she didn't realize how exhausted she was until now.

"So, did the police find anything more?" Lexy asked Jack over the rim of her wine glass.

"Looks like it was nothing but an unfortunate accident. I hope you're not blaming yourself."

Jack's eyes brimmed with concern. He gently picked up her left foot and put it in his lap, his forefinger and thumb working the tension in the arch.

Lexy frowned. "I hope they won't sue me or anything."

"First of all, no one even knows it was *you* that gave him the peanut sauce. The plates could have been moved or he ate out of someone's dish." Jack's fingers pressed on the points below her toes and Lexy felt herself relaxing back into the couch. "And second of all, the family didn't seem too upset about Regis' passing."

Lexy's radar pinged and she sat back up. "Really? Don't you find that suspicious that the family didn't care?"

Jack shrugged and started working on her other foot. "Not really. I mean, he was pretty old. They were all probably just waiting for him to die. As you can imagine, his kids will inherit a lot of money."

"But that's a perfect reason to kill him! Aren't you going to investigate any further?"

"Nope. We've determined there was no foul play."

"But his kids would benefit financially from his death," Lexy said incredulously.

"I know, but just because someone benefits from another's death doesn't always mean they murdered them. In this case we think it's unlikely because of his advanced age. He wasn't going to live much longer." Jack shrugged.

"I guess you're right," Lexy said. "Only a fool would take the risk of killing him if he was going to die on his own soon anyway, right?"

Chapter Four

Lexy rolled over in her bed, pulling the down comforter up to her chin. She snuggled into her pillow, sighing contentedly as a ray of sun warmed her cheek. She jerked her eyes open with a start—she was usually up well before the sun slid its rays through her window.

Rolling over in the bed, she noticed two things. Jack was already gone and the clock read seven thirty.

She was late!

Lexy bolted upright in the bed. Sprinkles followed her lead, leaping onto the floor, running in circles and then jumping back on the bed again.

Sliding her bare feet onto the hardwood floor, Lexy laughed at the antics of the little dog.

"Don't worry, Sprinkles, you'll get to show off in agility class later on today." Lexy smiled at Sprinkles, whose brown eyes gazed at her adoringly. The dog was full of energy and fast as a whip. Jack had come up with the idea of enrolling her in agility classes to help her work out some of her energy. Lexy didn't have visions of competing or anything, but it would be a great way to spend more time with the dog and give them both some much needed exercise.

But right now, Lexy had other things on her mind. Like hoping no one accused her of killing Regis Banks.

Grabbing the first tee-shirt and pair of jeans she could find, Lexy hopped into the shower. There was no time to wash her hair, so she coiled it into a ponytail set on the very top of her head, pulled tight so the hair flowed down like a fountain.

That doesn't look too bad for not washing it, she thought, as she gave herself a quick once-over in the mirror. She applied a swipe of mascara and some charcoal eye-liner to bring out the green in her eyes and she was good to go … except for shoes.

She grabbed a pair of wedges to add some height to her five-foot-four frame and headed downstairs, Sprinkles following obediently at her heels.

A quick glance at the grandfather clock in the living room told her that she'd gotten ready in record time. Still, she'd be later than usual getting to the bakery. Good thing it was her assistant, Cassie's, turn to open and start the baking.

Lexy poured some food into Sprinkles' bowl, shoved half an éclair into her mouth, slung her large tote bag over her shoulder and rushed out the door.

Clip-clopping down the drive-way toward her car, Lexy caught a strange movement out of the corner of her eye.

Were the tall shrubberies that lined the side of the driveway moving?

She stopped in her tracks, her heart thudding. Was someone hiding in the bushes? Who would do that in broad daylight?

"Who's there?" The éclair she was still chewing turned to ashes in her mouth when a body in a hooded sweatshirt stepped out from the bushes.

Lexy plunged her hand into her tote bag, her fingers frantically searching for the round canister of Mace.

"Stop right there!" She whipped the Mace out, pointing it at the intruder.

"Hey! Don't shoot!" The intruder held up both hands and Lexy noticed a pad of paper in one hand and a pen in the other. "Don't you recognize me? It's Norman Shea."

"Norman?" Lexy frowned at him. He pushed off the hood to reveal frizzy, carrot-red hair and a face that was almost completely hidden by large round tortoise framed eye-glasses.

With the hood off, Lexy recognized him. Norman Shea hadn't changed much since high school—he even still had the ever-present note-book in his hand. Lexy remembered Norman had been a little nerdy, not as popular as Lexy, and seemed to be always writing something.

"What are you doing lurking in my bushes?" Lexy asked.

"I'm with the Brook Ridge Tribune," Norman said pointing with pride to a laminated card hanging from his zipper.

"Oh, that's nice." Lexy glanced at her watch. "I'm kind of in a hurry—"

"I was hoping I could get a statement." Norman cut her off.

"Statement?"

"About the murder?"

"Murder?" Lexy narrowed her eyes at Norman.

"Regis Banks." Norman looked at her expectantly, his pen poised above the notepad.

"Regis wasn't murdered," Lexy bristled. "He died from a food allergy. I should know, I was there."

"I know." Norman said with obvious excitement. "I heard you served the fatal ice cream. I'm dubbing you the Killer Caterer—it should make for sensational headlines."

"What?" The word exploded from Lexy's mouth. She could practically feel her blood pressure rising and had to make a conscious effort to stop herself from spraying Norman with the Mace—the nerve of him!

Norman didn't seem to notice Lexy's fury. He was too busy scribbling in his notepad. "So, you deny it?"

"Deny it?" Lexy fought to compose herself. "There's nothing to deny. Regis' death was an accident."

"Right," Norman scribbled furiously. "An accident."

"Are you writing an article?"

Norman nodded, his eyes gleaming with excitement. "This is my big break. That's why I went to this trouble to get an exclusive with you."

Lexy stared at him incredulously. Didn't he realize that his big break could ruin her business?

"Norman Shea, I have nothing to say to you! In fact, you better leave right this instant or I'll tell your mother *you* were the one who put the firecrackers in the school toilets senior year!"

"You wouldn't!"

"Yes, I would." Even though it had been almost two decades ago, Lexy remembered the incident well. The water pipes had burst, causing a major flood. The school had been evacuated. No one ever discovered the culprit—except Lexy. Her detecting skills had been pretty good even back then. Of course, she'd never told anyone except

Norman. She wasn't a tattle-tale, but she wasn't above using it as a threat to get him to stop.

Norman's wide eyes looked from Lexy to his notepad and back again.

"Get!" Lexy shouted, pointing to the shrubs Norman had emerged from.

Norman snapped the cap on his pen. "All right. I'll leave, but you can't stop me from writing this story."

And then he disappeared back through the shrubs, leaving Lexy fuming in the driveway.

Lexy's heart sank as she slipped into her car. If Norman made good on his threat to write the article, it could put her out of business. She couldn't just sit around and hope things blew over.

Nope, it was in her best interest to take action to nip this whole thing in the bud and she knew the perfect people to help her—Nans and *The Ladies Detective Club*.

***

By the time Lexy got to the bakery, she'd calmed down. Maybe things weren't as bad as she thought. She didn't even know if the paper would publish Norman's article. It was purely speculation and she doubted the paper would want to open themselves to a lawsuit.

Cassie was taking something out of the oven when Lexy arrived and the tart aroma of lemons filled the air.

"Yum. That smells delicious!" Lexy eyed the lemon squares with their gooey, taste-bud puckering lemon peeking out from in-between the crust that had been crumbled on top.

"Hey, nice of you to come in today," Cassie teased, looking at the clock pointedly.

"Sorry, long night last night."

"I know, John filled me in. It's terrible what happened." Cassie's pierced eyebrows wrinkled with concern. "Are you okay?"

"Oh, yeah, I'm fine ... except Norman Shea showed up in my driveway this morning and wants to write an article about me. Says he's going to call me the Killer Caterer."

"What? He's a jerk." Cassie pulled a mixing bowl from the cabinet. "What are you going to do?"

"Well, Nans seemed eager to investigate the whole thing, so maybe she can help prove I didn't have anything to do with it."

"John said it was just an accident. Regis was old. Maybe he just forgot what bowl to eat from," Cassie offered. "Plus, I don't think you have to worry about Norman's article. There's nothing really to say and I doubt the paper is going to print something like that."

"Yeah, that's what I thought, too." Lexy chewed her bottom lip. "I'm positive I put the right ice cream in front of him. But if I didn't, I could have been the one that killed him."

"Now, don't go blaming yourself. It was an accident, like you said."

"Right." Lexy helped Cassie assemble the ingredients for the chocolate chip cookies they were making. Flour, sugar, vanilla extract, salt, chocolate chips, butter. She absently measured everything out, her mind more on Regis Banks' death than on baking. When she was done, Cassie pulled her aside.

"I can handle things here if you want to go talk to Nans."

"Oh, no. I feel bad leaving you."

"It's no problem. Haley will be in to help with the customers out front. Besides, I think you might do more harm than good here."

"Why?" Lexy frowned at Cassie.

"Because, I was watching you measure out the ingredients and you measured out two cups of salt instead of sugar."

***

"Lexy, what brings you here?" Nans stood in the doorway of her apartment at the *Brook Ridge Falls Retirement Center*, her brows raised at Lexy.

"For heaven's sake, Mona, can't you see she has a box of pastries?" Ida leaned back in her chair at the dining room table and nodded at the white bakery box Lexy balanced in the palm of her left hand. "Let her in."

"Oh, of course. Come in, dear." Nans stepped aside and Lexy entered the spacious apartment. As she suspected, Mona, Ida and Ruth were gathered around the dining room table with full cups of coffee and their iPads at the ready. Nans had already brought the large standing white-board from the spare room into the dining room so they could use it to write down suspects and clues.

"You're just in time," Ruth took the box from Lexy and peeked under the lid. "Oh, I love lemon squares."

Helen pulled out a chair and gestured for Lexy to sit. "Do you want some coffee? We were just discussing the Regis Banks case."

Lexy sat while the ladies busied themselves refreshing their coffees, getting small plates and selecting lemon squares. Nans put a steaming mug in front of Lexy and she sipped the brew, sighing as the caffeine made its way into her bloodstream.

"So, I take it you're going to join us in the investigation," Nans said to Lexy. "Last night, I got the impression you weren't too sure."

"That was before Norman Shea threatened to write an article dubbing me the Killer Caterer."

"What? Who is Norman Shea?" Ruth asked around a mouthful of lemon.

"He's a reporter for the Tribune and a former high school classmate," Lexy said. "He thinks this is some sort of big story that will launch his career."

"Oh, dear," Nans replied. "That can't be good for business."

"No kidding," Lexy said. "Anna's already called three times worried about this whole thing. Anyway, I figure it's best if we get to the bottom of how Regis got the wrong ice cream so I can clear myself of any wrong doing."

Helen broke off the edge of her lemon square. She'd picked an end piece as she usually did. She took a small nibble from the doughy end. "We haven't gotten very far … did you learn anything from Jack?"

"He said they didn't suspect foul play. They're ruling it an accident and aren't going to investigate any further."

"Really?" Nans face puckered. "With all that money involved, I don't see how they can say that."

"He said that because Regis was so old anyway, it doesn't make sense that someone would take the risk of killing him. Odds are he didn't have much time left."

"Good point." Nans rubbed her palms together to rid them of crumbs and stood at the whiteboard, taking a big marker in her hand. "Well, let's get started with what we know."

"I scoured the tabloids and there's not one whiff of a girlfriend," Ruth said.

"So I guess we can rule out a jealous lover," Ida giggled.

"The next logical place to look is at the family," Helen said. "I assume his children would gain financially from his death."

"One would think." Nans wrote Winston, Lawrence and Olivia on the white board. "Ruth, did you pick up anything interesting on either of them?"

"It seems Winston was cut from the same cloth as Regis. A tough businessman. He is a vice president at *Banks Development*, Regis' company. It's said they were tough negotiators and would do anything to win a deal."

"What does the company do?" Lexy asked.

"Commercial real estate development. Big stuff like malls and office buildings."

"Go on, Ruth," Nans prompted.

"Lawrence, on the other hand, was the opposite. Hates big business and is very ecology minded. He opposed a lot of the company's business plans. He thought they were ruining the planet by turning fields and forests into buildings and parking lots."

"Interesting," Nans wrote under Lawrence's name. "So, do you think he hated what the company did enough to kill his father?"

Ruth shrugged. "Who knows? It's certainly something to look into."

"What about the daughter?" Ida asked over the rim of her dainty china coffee cup.

Ruth looked down at her iPad. "She doesn't seem to be interested in the company too much. Your typical rich girl socialite, going to parties and dressing in expensive clothes. Has the usual upper class hobbies, the latest of which seems to be raising dogs."

Lexy remembered Olivia's expensive clothes and shoes at the party. "Seems like she already has a lot of money, judging by the way she dressed. I doubt she'd kill her father for money."

"Well, that depends." Nans turned to face them. "We don't know what kind of money she has and if her needs outstrip what she makes."

"Does she even have a job?" Helen asked.

"No. Just expensive hobbies."

"So she must have been living off of Daddy's money." Ida took another lemon square from the box. "We know Winston worked at the company, but what about Lawrence?"

"Believe it or not, Lawrence works at the Farmer's Market. He's a manager."

"What?" Nans scrunched up her face. "That can't pay very well for a multi-millionaire's son."

"I'm sure it doesn't," Ruth said. "But maybe he gets an allowance from Regis to supplement his income, just like Olivia."

Nans pursed her lips and tapped them with the end of the marker. "I heard Regis was a mis-er—maybe that allowance wasn't enough."

"But would one of them kill him because of that? Like Jack said, he was one-hundred already. How much longer could he live?" Lexy asked.

"Good point." Nans said. "That means it would have to be someone with an immediate need for the money."

"Right," Ruth agreed. "Someone who couldn't wait for Regis to die."

"And given his advanced age, they probably figured that if they fed him peanut butter everyone would assume he died of natural causes and there would be no investigation," Helen added.

"As far as we know, only three people would benefit financially from Regis' death," Nans said pointing to the three names on the whiteboard. "We just need to figure out which one of them needed money so badly that they'd murder their own father for it."

Chapter Five

Lexy thought about Nans' theory later that day as she drove with Sprinkles to the *Fur Fun K9 Center*. Would one of Regis' kids really have killed him to get their inheritance? The thought made Lexy shudder. As if sensing her thoughts, Sprinkles whined in the passenger seat, giving Lexy a worried look.

"It's okay, Sprinkles. We're going to have fun at agility class." She reached over and scratched the dog behind the ears.

Lexy turned her mind to happier thoughts. The death of Regis at the party hadn't affected her sales at the bakery one bit. In fact, Lexy had been so busy ringing up sales after she'd gotten back to the bakery from Nans that she'd worked late and had to rush home.

"Hopefully we won't be late for the class," Lexy said to Sprinkles as she turned onto Meadow Road, the dirt country road that ran out to the *K9 Center*.

Glancing up into the rear-view mirror, Lexy noticed a car had pulled onto the desolate road behind her. An old, beige Plymouth Sundance. Uneasiness pricked her stomach. She'd seen that car somewhere before.

Sprinkles was looking out the window, focused on the passing scenery. She stood on hind legs with her front paws on the arm rest, her nose making wet marks on the glass. Suddenly she erupted in a chorus of barks, pulling Lexy's attention away from the car behind her.

"What is it?" Lexy looked in the direction of Sprinkles' attention, but all she could see were large fields and woods. The area was completely undeveloped. The fields, once lush with rows of vegetables, were now overgrown, but still had a peaceful beauty to them. A rabbit hopped along an old stone wall. Birds flitted in the twisted branches of the rugged old oak trees that lined the property. A rundown farmhouse and barn sat off in the distance, their roofs sagging with age. A tree grew out of one of the farmhouse windows, a sad reminder of the progress of the times.

Lexy didn't see any movement. The place looked like it had been abandoned for decades, so she had no idea what had attracted Sprinkles attention.

She glanced back up at the rear-view mirror. The road behind her was empty. The Sundance had turned off. Lexy relaxed, laughing at herself.

All this talk of murder had her afraid of her own shadow.

She turned a corner and the big sign for the *K9 Center* came into view.

"We're almost there," she announced to Sprinkles, who wagged her tail happily.

She parked and got out, coming round to the passenger side to take hold of Sprinkle's leash and lead her into the parking lot. The setting sun cast long shadows from the trees. She could hear the peepers chirping in the fields that surrounded the facility. Lexy inhaled a deep breath of country air. There was nothing like being in the middle of nowhere, and this place surely was.

She checked Sprinkles' harness and headed for the main door.

The facility was gigantic. Lexy had heard it was the largest indoor agility facility on the East Coast. They hosted many competitions, but also had a dog grooming center, doggy day-care and a boarding facility. She followed the signs for the agility class, her mouth hanging open in awe as the path led her to a giant stadium. She'd had no idea a big facility like this existed way out here.

Several people were clustered to the left of the door with their dogs. Lexy figured she'd found the agility class. She trotted over, introduced herself and took her place in between a hyped up Jack

Russell Terrier and a more sedate, medium sized black and white mixed breed. Sprinkles made friends with the dogs, while Lexy did the same with their owners.

Agility training turned out to be a lot harder than Lexy thought it would be. After the instructor showed them the various pieces of equipment and explained how they were used, she put the dogs—and owners—through a short agility course that left Lexy gasping for air. She was glad when the break came, although Sprinkles, who seemed to be in better shape than Lexy, acted like she could have run the course all night.

In her mad rush from the bakery, Lexy hadn't brought any water and the activity had made her thirsty, so she headed off in search of a vending machine. Following the signs to the refreshment area, she must have taken a wrong turn because she found herself in a darkened maze of hallways that didn't look like they were part of the main facility.

This probably leads to the offices and storage, she thought. She started to turn back, but then hushed voices coming from one of the hallways caught her attention.

"We can't let anyone find out!" The woman's voice piqued Lexy's natural curiosity.

"Shhh. You don't want anyone to hear us." This from a man in the same hushed tones.

Lexy flattened herself against the wall and slid toward the hallway opening where the voices were coming from. She strained to hear, inching closer, but they were talking in whispers now.

Sprinkles sat on the floor in front of Lexy, her head tilted to one side, her ears moving like tiny radar dishes. She sniffed the air. Once. Twice. Then her eyes slid over to the hallway and she took off at full speed, jerking the leash out of Lexy's hand.

"Sprinkles. Come back!" Lexy tried to step on the end of the leash before it disappeared into the hall, but Sprinkles was too quick. Lexy lunged into the hallway, diving for the leash.

"Farfel!" The woman's voice, this time tight with panic.

At the end of the leash, Sprinkles rolled around the floor with a small ball of orange fur. Was it a dog? Lexy could hardly tell. The fur must have been a foot thick.

From her crouched position, Lexy could tell the dogs were just playing. She tugged the leash. "Sprinkles! Come!"

A pair of Jimmy Choo stiletto's skidded around the corner. Lexy recognized those shoes. Her gaze drifted upwards, her eyes confirming who was attached to them. Olivia Banks. And she was running toward them with an unpleasant scowl on her face. Behind Olivia, Lexy could just make out the broad shoulders of a man with longish, dark curly hair disappear down the other side of the hall.

Olivia zoned in on the orange fur ball and scooped it up in her arms.

"Farfel! Are you all right? Don't scare Mommy by taking off like that, you naughty girl!" She held the dog out at arm's length, apparently inspecting it for damage.

"I think they were only playing," Lexy said as she reeled Sprinkles in.

Olivia looked in her direction, her impossibly blue eyes narrowing. "You look familiar. Do I know you?"

"Sort of." Lexy stuck out her hand. "I'm Lexy Baker, I was one of the caterers at your father's birthday party the other night.

Lexy's composure wilted under Olivia's glare. Maybe she shouldn't have mentioned the party. Did Olivia think Lexy had been the one that screwed up and served Regis peanut sauce? Lexy pulled Sprinkles closer, ready to make a hasty retreat if the other woman took offense.

Olivia surprised her by tucking the orange fur ball under her arm and accepting Lexy's handshake. "I'm Olivia Banks ... but I guess you already knew that."

Olivia's handshake was cold and firm. Lexy's gaze drifted to the dog. A small, foxlike face peered out from inside a large puff of fur. The dog almost seemed to be smiling at Lexy. "Your dog is such a cutie."

"Oh, thanks. She's a Pomeranian with keen agility skills. I think she could be a show-dog as well, don't you?"

Lexy nodded and Olivia slid her eyes toward Sprinkles.

"Oh, this is Sprinkles. She's a Poodle Shih-Tzu mix," Lexy said. "We're doing the agility class, but just for fun. Do you compete?"

"I should say so." Olivia nodded. Her perfectly cut blonde bob swayed like silk. "We've won lots of awards."

"Congratulations." Up close, Lexy could see the woman had crow's feet and neck lines that belied her age, though she did have to admit she looked pretty good for sixty. Even so, she probably owed a lot of that to expensive skin creams, Botox and Juviderm. She must have to spend a lot of money to keep her face looking so youthful.

Olivia smiled proudly, then her gaze turned suspicious. "What are you doing down *here,* though. The agility class is clear on the other side of the building."

"I must have gotten lost. I worked up quite a thirst in class. I was looking for a vending machine."

"The vending machines are that way." Olivia thrust her chin toward the hallway Lexy had come down, then glanced behind her. "Come on, I'll show you the way."

Lexy followed Olivia into the hall, admiring the other woman's silk shirt and designer jeans. This was probably her grunge outfit and it cost more than Lexy's entire wardrobe.

"I'm sorry about your father." Lexy couldn't pass up the opportunity to get any information she could from Olivia. She realized even the most innocently seeming piece of information could lead to a clue about who would want Regis dead. "Did he have agility dogs, too?"

Olivia snorted. "Daddy? Are you kidding? If it didn't have to do with constructing some monstrous building, he didn't want to know about it."

"Well, I'm sure you'll miss him," Lexy ventured as they turned down another hallway.

Olivia's face hardened. "Daddy barely noticed me. He had more in common with Winston, even if Win was acting like a jerk lately and had that strange fear of germs."

"Germs?"

"Yes, always washing his hands and using those towelettes after he touches anything. He can't stand my dogs, says they're loaded with germs."

"You said he was acting like a jerk … I noticed he did seem strange at the party," Lexy said.

Olivia glanced at her. "Yes. He's starting to take after Daddy, I'm afraid. Bad temper and such. His poor wife suffers the brunt of it—just like my mother did. Maybe that's why Daddy seemed to like him best. Probably left everything to him, too."

"Oh, I doubt that. I mean, surely he would have divided it up evenly?"

Olivia shrugged. "Maybe. Daddy was all about *the business*. He didn't approve of my dogs and he and Larry certainly didn't get along. I mean, Larry is about as anti-business as they come. It was Winston that he was closest with."

"But I'm sure he loved you all the same."

"Daddy let Winston live in an estate property the family owns. I was lucky to get a small town-house and a yearly stipend." She waved her hand in the air. "It was barely enough to keep my Poms in kibble."

"Oh, so your family wasn't close?" Lexy asked as they came to the end of the hall.

49

"We used to be close back when Mother was alive. Those were good days. But now ..." Her eyes got glassy as she let her voice trail off, then she sucked in a breath and waved her hand. "Well, one can't wish for things that aren't going to happen. Besides, dogs make better family than any humans, don't you think?"

Lexy looked down at Sprinkles. "I can't argue with that."

"Well, here are the vending machines." Olivia gestured to the far side of the room where a bank of machines sat. "Nice to meet you, and good luck with your agility training."

Lexy watched Olivia clackety-clack away on her stilettos. She certainly didn't seem upset about her father's death. But if she really didn't think he would leave her much money, she would have had no reason to kill him.

Lexy doubted Regis left all the money to Winston, though. What father would leave money to just one kid?

Olivia must be getting a tidy sum despite what she implied. There seemed to be no love lost between Olivia and Daddy. And if her allowance wasn't enough to keep her dogs in kibble and her feet in Jimmy Choo's, maybe she finally got fed up and killed him.

Chapter Six

Lexy pulled up in front of the *Brook Ridge Falls Retirement Center* bright and early the next morning. Nans, Ruth, Ida and Helen were waiting just outside the front door with colorful spring blouses on, their giant purses dangling from their arms.

The morning sun reflected off the glass doors as the women walked toward her car. It was almost nine o'clock and Lexy should have been elbow deep in flour at the bakery, but Nans had plans to talk to Lawrence Banks today and Lexy couldn't resist tagging along. Plus, she couldn't wait to tell the ladies about her talk with Olivia.

Helen opened the back door and gestured for Ruth and Ida to pile in. Lexy marveled at how the three ladies could fold themselves into the tiny backseat of her Volkswagen.

"Hurry up, Ruth. We haven't got all day." Ida shoved Ruth from behind.

"Hey, watch it," Ruth yelled over her shoulder as she navigated the backseat. "I strained something on my side in yoga last night. Give me a break."

"I told you not to try that sideways crane pose," Nans admonished, sliding into the passenger seat.

"What? You think you're the only one that can do that pose?" Ruth's eyes challenged Nans' in the rear view mirror.

"What's the sideways crane pose?" Lexy asked while Ida and Helen took their places in the back.

"Oh, never mind that," Nans said. "It's just a yoga pose. I'm more interested in hearing what you learned from Olivia."

Lexy pulled out onto the main drag, telling them about the hushed conversation she'd overheard and how Olivia wasn't close to her father and admitted that Regis barely gave her enough to live on.

"That sounds like motive right there," Ida said.

"Yeah, but she seemed to think Regis didn't leave her very much in the will. She claimed Winston would get most of it."

"I wonder if that's true," Nans said. "We need to find out what's in the will."

"I'm on that," Ruth chimed in from the back seat. "I have a call into my friend, Shirley Russell. She works for Greenburg, Lewis, Morgan and Slate."

"Who?" Ida looked sideways at Ruth, her brows dipped in a wrinkly 'V'.

"That's the law firm Regis Banks used. She said she'd be willing to take a peek at the will for a dozen éclairs." Ruth tapped Lexy on the shoulder. "Can you whip those up?"

"Sure." Lexy made a mental note to bake extra éclairs when she got to the bakery later on.

"Olivia could just be saying that, too," Ida added. "You know, to make it look like she didn't have a motive."

"Well, she *was* sitting next to him." Lexy turned into the Farmer's Market parking lot.

"And Winston was on his other side," Nans added. "If what Olivia said is true and Winston is getting most everything, then I'm putting my money on him."

"Well, let's see what Lawrence says." Lexy pulled into a parking spot. "Just how do you plan to get him to talk to us, anyway?"

"Oh, that's easy," Nans said, unhooking her seatbelt and opening the door. "People love to talk to old ladies. We'll just tell him we're friends of his father."

The Farmer's Market took place in a large warehouse type building. It was a fairly new en-deavor that featured local food combined with organic items sourced from other areas. Today, it bustled with activity.

Lexy scanned the interior which consisted of various stands much the same as you'd find in an outdoor market.

"Over there." Ruth pointed to the left and Lexy recognized Lawrence in a black tee-shirt and khaki pants, hefting watermelons onto a display cart. She calculated his age at late sixties, but he still seemed quite spry.

Nans led the way past displays of colorful produce resting on chipped ice, barrels of dried fruit and a section of grind-your-own organic coffee beans that smelled like heaven.

Lawrence noticed the five of them marching toward him when they were about five feet away. "Can I help you?"

"Yes, aren't you Lawrence Banks?" Nans asked.

Lawrence's brows rose in surprise. "I am, but everyone calls me Larry."

"Okay, Larry. I'm Mona and this is Ruth, Ida, Helen and my granddaughter, Lexy." Nans pointed out each of them in turn. "We were friends of your Dad's and wanted to come to pay our respects."

"Oh, thanks." Larry brushed his hands throughout his crew cut and narrowed his eyes at

Nans. "You ladies look awfully young to be friends of my father's."

Nans blushed and patted her short, gray curls. "Why, thank you. I know he was a lot older, but we knew him from senior activities."

"We were at his birthday party," Ruth said.

"That must have been awful for you." Helen turned watery eyes on Larry and his face softened.

"Yes, it was," Larry said. "But he *was* one-hundred years old and there are worse ways to go. He lived long enough."

"Sounds like you and your father didn't get along," Ida said.

"Well, as you know, he was all about corporate profits no matter what the cost. I just didn't share his views. I'm about saving the planet." Larry spread his arms, gesturing out into the store. "I try to do what I can here to help promote local foods and organic growing practices. Do you realize that if we keep up the way we are, we'll ruin the whole earth?"

Lexy noticed the obvious passion in Larry's voice. "So you never wanted to work for *Banks Development* like Winston?"

"No. If Winston and Father had their way, they'd pave the whole planet."

"But, surely you would have made a lot of money working there," Nans said.

"Oh, sure, I'd make a lot more money. But I don't care about money. I live a simple life. Heck, Dad even tried to get me to live in one of the buildings on his estate, but I prefer to rent my cabin in the woods. Winston, on the other hand … well, let's just say he liked the money."

"I've heard. You two sure are different for brothers," Nans said.

"I'll say." Larry's lips tightened into a thin line and his eyes glazed into a faraway look. "Dad gave all of us an allowance, but I donated mine to causes that help the planet. Winston spent his and then some."

"And then some?" Nans prompted.

Larry's eyes cleared and he shook his head. "Winston used to be a good guy but lately he seems to have lost his way."

"What do you mean?" Nans persisted.

"Fell into a bad habit, I guess." Larry glanced at the floor, his face a tide of emotions. "The whole family seems to have drifted apart and I just wish we could all be closer, even if we do have our differences. Maybe then I could help him—"

"Larry, are these on sale—" A woman had walked up, her eyes on a bunch of arugula she held in her hand. She stopped abruptly when she looked up and saw Larry talking to the group. "Oh, sorry, I didn't realize … do I know you?"

Lexy narrowed her eyes. She recognized the red-head from the birthday party—it was Winston's wife! But she looked different now—happy.

"Do you know my sister-in-law, Evelyn?" Larry asked, then turned to Evelyn. "These are friends of Dad's. They were at the party."

"Oh, right. I thought they looked familiar." She smiled and nodded a greeting.

"You work here?" Nans narrowed her eyes at Evelyn.

"Why, yes." Evelyn glanced at Larry, looking a bit taken aback at the incredulous tone of Nans' voice. "I'm trying to help support local farmers—the few we have left anyway—and support organic farming and earth safe practices."

"Oh, sorry. I just thought with your husband being a vice president over at Banks Development …" Nans let the sentence trial off.

Evelyn's face grew hard at the mention of Winston. She tugged at the sleeve of her tee-shirt and Lexy noticed a bruise on her arm. Olivia's words about Evelyn suffering the brunt of Winston's temper came back to her. Had Winston been hitting Evelyn?

"One doesn't have to share all the same values as one's husband. I'm not as keen on developing every piece of land into a mall as Winston is." Evelyn turned to Larry and held up the arugula. "Sorry to interrupt. I was just wondering if I should put the sale sign on these."

"Yes, those are on sale." Larry turned to Nans and the ladies. "We're having a big sale today. In fact, we're practically giving away organic raspberries over there. Why don't you check them out?"

Larry pushed Nans gently toward a cart loaded with plump dark-pink berries.

"Okay. Thanks." Nans started reluctantly toward the cart. Lexy knew Nans wanted to ask more questions, but was smart enough to know when she was being dismissed. No sense in being too aggressive and making him suspicious.

They walked over to the cart and Lexy picked up a pint of plump berries. Just the sight of them made her mouth water, especially when she envisioned them baked into scones. She inspected the pint with one eye, keeping the other eye on Larry and Winston's wife, Evelyn, who had their heads together in the corner, whispering and smiling.

"Well, that was enlightening," Nans whispered as she squeezed a tangerine.

"It was?" Ruth held a cantaloupe up to her ear and tapped the side. "It doesn't seem like Larry would be the killer. You heard him … he doesn't care about money."

"Not Larry," Nans said. "Winston. If you read between the lines, Larry was clearly saying that Winston has a big problem. And that problem could be behind the murder. We just need to find out what it is."

***

"How are we going to find out Winston's secret?" Ruth asked from the backseat of Lexy's car as they drove back to the retirement center.

"Simple, we'll ask someone who knows him," Nans replied.

"Who?" Helen asked.

"At the party it looked like he and the wife weren't getting along," Lexy said.

"Ha! See, all the more reason to believe he was up to something."

"But we can't ask his wife." Ida chewed her bottom lip. "We need to find someone we know in common."

"That's a good idea," Nans said. "Ruth, you work your magic on the internet. Find out every charity and board that Winston was on. I'm sure

59

between the five of us we'll find someone we know."

"What about Olivia?" Lexy took a left into the retirement center parking lot. "It seemed like she had a secret, too."

"Yes, we shouldn't discount her." Nans unhooked her seatbelt as Lexy pulled up to the front of the building. "Maybe you can try to find out more at the next agility class? If you befriend her, you could get the inside scoop."

Lexy frowned at Nans. "I hardly think we'd be good friends. She's too 'high society'."

"But you have a love of dogs in common," Helen reminded her as she slid out of the backseat.

Lexy thought about Norman Shea and his threat to write the article. If making friends with Olivia would help find out what really happened with the ice cream, then she'd have to do it. "Okay, I'll see what I can do."

"Great!" Nans hopped out of the passenger seat.

Ida slid out of the back with Ruth right behind her. Ruth leaned her head in as she turned to shut the door.

"And Lexy," she said. "You better get baking those éclairs today. I'll be seeing Shirley tomorrow at noon so we can find out what's really in the will."

Chapter Seven

"I need to bake an extra batch of éclairs today. Do you think we can fit it in?" Lexy asked Cassie who was bent-over the stove, retrieving a baking sheet full of peanut butter cookies.

"Sure. We can do those next." Cassie squatted down and opened one of the bottom cabinets, her blonde spiked hair sticking up from behind the door. "And you can tell me what's going on with the Regis Banks death."

Lexy's stomach clenched. "Why? Did you hear something?"

"No." Cassie retrieved a large, stainless steel bowl and put it on the marble topped island in the center of the room. "I was just wondering how it was going."

"Oh. I was afraid Norman had written that article."

"He hasn't. I asked my cousin down at the paper and she said he told her he was working on something secret but still had to chase down some facts." Cassie grabbed milk, eggs and unsalted butter from the fridge.

Lexy brought over the sugar, cornstarch and a vanilla bean. She split the bean down the length.

The scent of vanilla perfumed the air. She carefully scraped the seeds out of the bean pod while she filled Cassie in on her talks with Olivia and Lawrence.

"So you think Winston did it?" Cassie held out the saucepan full of milk and Lexy scraped the seeds in.

"He was sitting next to Regis. He could have easily switched the ice cream bowls." Lexy separated the yolks from the eggs into a bowl and added sugar, double checking to make sure it *was* sugar and not salt and started beating.

"You really think he would kill his own father?" Cassie shuddered as she stirred the milk mixture.

Lexy shrugged. "People do drastic things when they need money."

"True dat." Cassie removed the pan from the stove just as the bells chimed out in the store part of the bakery.

"Is it my turn?" Lexy asked. When the shop wasn't busy, the girls spent their time in the kitchen, each taking turns when a customer came in.

"Yep."

Lexy wiped her hands on a kitchen towel and straightened her pink-cupcake pattern apron before heading toward the opening that led to the front of the store.

George Finley stood in front of the glass pastry case, bent over slightly, looking in at the muffins. He looked up as Lexy approached the case, a smile on his lips.

"Hey ya, Lexy."

"Hi, George. What can I get for you today?"

"Well, I'm trying to make up my mind." His blue eyes sparkled beneath white, bushy brows. George was a regular, coming in once a week for a supply of baked goods. "Everything looks so good."

"Thanks." Lexy beamed at the compliment, standing patiently behind the case while George looked over the assortment of muffins, cookies, bars, cakes and scones. The smell of coffee from the self-serve station in the corner wafted over and Lexy felt a pang in her stomach—she could sure use a cup.

"Let me know when you've decided." Lexy grabbed a clean dish towel and headed over to the coffee station, wiping it clean and then pouring a steaming mug for herself.

Turning around, she surveyed the cafe tables she had set up next to the window for customers who wanted to linger over coffee and pastry. They were spotless, but she wiped them down anyway, mostly out of habit.

Lexy felt a swell of pride as she glanced out of the floor-to-ceiling storefront window at the view of the waterfall across the street. The view was one of the things that had sold her on this space in the old mill building. It had taken years of hard work to get this far. She couldn't let that one incident with Regis Banks ruin everything.

A blur of beige went by and something niggled Lexy's memory. Was that the car that she'd seen behind her on the way to the agility class?

"I heard about Regis Banks," George said as if reading her mind. Lexy's stomach sank. She turned to look at him, forgetting about the beige car. If word had gotten out already, people might avoid the bakery.

"Yeah, that was awful," she said.

"Awful? I think it was about time."

"Excuse me?" Lexy's brows knit together. She walked back toward the case, staring at George.

"Oh, I know it sounds mean, but I'm glad the old goat is dead."

"Really? You didn't like him?"

"Not too many did."

"Why?"

George frowned. "He might have been a good businessman, but he was a terrible person. Do you know how he came by all the land that made him rich?"

66

Lexy shook her head. "Not really. I just assumed he bought it."

"Bought it? He stole it. Ripped it right out from under poor, unsuspecting folks. Hard working folks like you and me."

"Stole it? But how could he—"

"I don't mean he did anything illegal. No, he was too smart for that. He skirted right along the edge of the law. Preyed on families in distress and worked them until they sold the land at dirt cheap prices." George pressed his lips together and shook his head. "Used some sneaky, underhanded tricks too."

"I never heard that."

"Well, most people don't like to talk about it. The families it happened to were probably embarrassed. But if you ask me, there are a lot of people who wanted him dead, even if he was already old. Some would have loved the satisfaction of doing him in themselves." George shrugged, then tapped on the glass front of the case. "I'll take a half dozen of those raspberry scones."

Lexy boxed up the scones, her mind whirling as she cashed George out and bid him goodbye. She hadn't considered that Regis might have an enemy that would want him dead. But, again, who would go to the trouble of killing a one-hundred year old man?

Her phone chirped and she pulled it out of her pocket. Nans.

"Hi, Lexy. Can you put together a box of assorted pastries for tomorrow morning?"

"Sure. Why?"

"Ruth discovered that Winston Banks serves on the same charity board with Stanley McKitterick. We know Stan. In fact, he's kind of sweet on Helen."

"I made a discovery of my own today," Lexy said. She searched the pastry case deciding what to put in the box.

"Oh, really?"

"Yep. George Finley was in and he told me that Regis was a little sketchy in his business dealings."

"I'd heard he was a tough businessman."

"Well, according to George, he screwed people over. He seems to think there would be plenty of people who would have liked to have seen Regis dead."

"Revenge. I didn't think of that," Nans said.

Lexy could hear the squeak of marker on white-board through the phone. "I'll write that down, but it would have had to be someone at the party and I doubt anyone who had a grudge against Regis would have been invited. Besides, how would they have gotten close enough to switch the ice cream?"

"Good point." Lexy felt disappointed. "I guess the Winston angle is the best we have so far."

"Right. We're meeting with Stan at eleven tomorrow. Do you want to come with us?"

***

Of course, Lexy wanted to go with Nans and the ladies to meet with Stan, so she picked them up at ten thirty and drove to the ritzy neighborhood where Stan lived. His expansive Cape Cod house was situated on a large, well-landscaped lot. Stan didn't have as much money as Winston Banks, but he seemed to be fairly well off.

They walked to the door and Nans pushed Helen to the front, then rang the bell.

The door opened.

"Helen!" A man of about eighty answered the door, his tanned face breaking into a wide smile at Helen. His sharp brown eyes looked over her shoulder at the rest of us, lighting with recognition when they fell on Nans, Ruth and Ida. "Ladies, how nice to see you."

"It's always a pleasure, Stanley." Nans grabbed the box of pastries from Lexy and held them up. "My granddaughter, Lexy, brought some pastries from her bakery."

"Oh, right. You own *The Cup and Cake* don't you?"

"Yes, that's right."

"Nice to meet you." Stan pushed the door wide. "Please, come in and join me. I was just about to have a cup of tea."

They followed Stan down an oak paneled hallway to the wide country kitchen. A red brick fireplace dominated one wall, birch cabinets on the rest.

"Have a seat." Stan gestured toward a solid maple table and chair set as he got busy transferring the pastries from the box to a large crystal platter. Lexy and the ladies arranged themselves at the table, forcing Helen into the seat to the right of the chair at the head of the table, which they left empty for Stan.

"Tea?" Stan turned with a steaming teapot in his hand. They all murmured yes and a few minutes later each of them had their teacups full and pastries on small etched crystal plates in front of them.

"So, to what do I owe this pleasure?" Stan plucked a sugar cube out of a bowl with silver tongs and dropped it into his tea.

"Well, it's kind of a delicate matter." Helen leaned into Stan and smiled up at him from beneath her lashes. Lexy noticed Stan got all googly-eyed. The man was positively smitten with Helen.

"Go on," he sighed.

"Well, you see," Helen cleared her throat. "I have some questions about Winston Banks."

"Banks? Oh, yes, I know the fellow." Stan gazed into Helen's eyes. Lexy wondered if he even knew what he was saying.

Lexy, Nans, Ruth and Ida sipped their tea and nibbled their pastries in silence—no one wanted to say a word for fear they would break the spell Helen seemed to have cast over Stan.

"I'm writing a piece for the paper about old money and how it affects the second generation," Helen said, casting a nervous glance at the others.

Nans left eyebrow ticked up, but she didn't say a word.

"Oh, you still write for the paper?" Stanley asked.

"Sometimes." Helen sipped her tea. "Anyway, you know how money can corrupt. I was just wondering if Winston was corrupted by the Banks millions."

Stan scrunched up his face, chewing on his bottom lip like he knew something and was deciding whether or not to tell. Helen leaned in even closer, smiling even wider. Lexy wondered if she would actually go so far as to bat her eyelashes.

"Well, I suppose this isn't a big secret, so I don't think I'm talking out of school. Winston was a pretty good guy, but he did have one weakness."

"Oh?"

"Gambling. He was into poker big time. Too bad he wasn't a very good player. Heck, I even cleaned him out a few times and I'm only a fair player. But, with his money ..." Stan shrugged.

"Oh, so did he play often or was it just in friendly weekly games?" Helen asked.

"At first, he just played a casual weekly game. But then I heard he got in deep. Started going to some high stakes games in the city. I guess there's a whole underground poker network that plays in the back rooms of seedy bars." Stan shook his head. "That's a real nasty crowd. A man could get in big trouble if he lost a lot of money. But, with Winston's money he had a lot to play with.

"Yes, he did have a lot," Helen agreed.

Nans exchanged looks with Lexy. Did he have a lot of money? Rumor had it Regis kept them on a tight budget, but he must have made a good salary.

"So, anyway, Helen, how have you been?" Stan slid his hand on top of hers. "It's been a long time."

"Yes, too long. And it's been lovely to see you again." Helen slid her hand out from under Stan's. "But we really must be going."

"So soon?"

"Yes, I'm afraid Ida has an appointment at the podiatrist at noon and she really can't miss it." Helen leaned closer to Stan and whispered loudly, "Her toenails are like horse hoofs."

Nans, Ruth and Lexy stifled giggles while Ida shot daggers at Helen. They pushed up from their chairs, murmured their thanks and had a round of good-byes at the door before escaping to the car.

"That explains it. Winston really did have an urgent need for the money." Nans half-turned in her seat to look at Ruth, Ida and Helen.

"Some of those gamblers are bad news. If he owed a lot of money, they could have threatened him with all kinds of nasty things," Ida said.

"And I'm sure he couldn't go to his father for money," Lexy added.

Ruth snorted. "No way. Regis wouldn't approve of gambling."

"But if Regis died," Helen said, "then Winston might inherit enough to pay off the gambling debt."

"We *think* he would," Ida leaned forward, sticking her head into the front seat. "We won't know for sure until Ruth talks to Shirley about the will."

"I don't know about you girls, but this puts Winston at the top of the suspect list for me." Nans blue eyes twinkled with excitement. "If we can find out how much he owed, we might be able to prove that he had a motive and maybe the police would open it as a homicide and clear Lexy of any wrongdoing."

"And just how do you propose we do that?" Lexy slid a sideways glance at her grandmother, picturing the four ladies crashing high stakes poker games disguised in matching tan trench coats.

"Oh, I'm not exactly sure right now ... but I'll think of something," Nans said.

"That's *exactly* what I'm afraid of," Lexy replied.

Chapter Eight

Lexy had to admit she was worried about Nans and the ladies doing something crazy in order to find out about the poker games. She figured she better try to head them off at the pass and get the information herself. And she couldn't think of anyone who would know more about the seedy world of underground high stakes poker games than her own husband.

She took a coconut cream pie home from the bakery. It was Jack's favorite dessert—she hoped that would persuade him to be more talkative about the poker games. She figured a nice home-cooked meal wouldn't hurt either, which was why she'd left work a little early and picked up the fixings for lasagna.

Lexy stood in the kitchen, one eye on the clock and the other on the oven where the lasagna was just now browning. Jack should be home in ten minutes. The timing was perfect to get the meal to the table just as he walked in the door.

Sprinkles watched her with hawk-like eyes as she mixed the salad.

"You want a little piece of lettuce?"

Sprinkles spun around gleefully. Lexy picked a piece of romaine out of the bowl and handed it to the dog who sniffed it, swallowed it in one gulp and then returned to staring up at Lexy.

She heard Jack's car pull into the driveway and her stomach flip-flopped. Even though they'd been married almost a year, Jack still had that effect on her. She poured red wine into two wine glasses, then leaned against the counter with one glass held out as Jack walked into the room.

"Hey, now, that's how I like to be greeted." He took the glass and kissed her on the lips, then glanced at the oven. "What's the occasion?"

"Oh, nothing." Lexy opened the oven door to a perfect lasagna—the edges just turning golden. "I thought a good meal would be fun."

"Well, you know I always like a good meal."

"You sit. I'll serve." Lexy pushed him toward the table.

"Oh, and I get waited on?" Jack sipped his wine. "Doesn't get much better than that."

"Don't worry, you can do the dishes." Lexy slid the lasagna out of the oven and put it on top of the stove to cool while she tossed the salad, then scooped some into matching teak salad bowls. She slid one bowl in front of Jack, then took the seat opposite him.

"So, how was work?" Lexy speared a cherry tomato and brought it to her lips.

"The usual." Jack replied. "You?"

"Great. I brought home coconut cream pie for dessert."

Jack's eyes lit at the mention of his favorite pie. "Yum. After dessert, we should do some more packing at my house."

Lexy picked through her salad. Jack lived in the house behind her. In fact, they'd met initially when Sprinkles slipped through a gap in the fence and did her 'business' on Jacks shrubs. Shortly after, he'd had to accuse her of murdering her ex-fiancé, but it had all worked out in the end and now they were one married couple with two houses.

Lexy had refused to part with the house she'd bought from Nans—it had too many wonderful childhood memories. So, they'd decided to put Jack's house up for sale. But first, they'd have to clean it out and get it ready. The house was packed to the brim with 'stuff', some of it from the previous owners who had lived there for over fifty years. It was proving to be a daunting task.

Lexy got up and cut the lasagna. She put a large, gooey, cheesy-dripping piece on on Jack's plate and a smaller one on her own. She sat back down and concentrated on eating while contemplating how to divert the conversation to high stakes gambling.

"Did you hear anything more from Norman Shea?" Jack asked.

Lexy had told him about Norman accosting her in the driveway. Jack had offered to talk to him and make sure he didn't bother her again, but Lexy had developed a pang of sympathy for the nerdy Norman and declined. The police visiting him would probably scar him for life.

"No, but Nans has been digging into the Regis Banks death," she ventured.

Jack's eyebrows rose and Lexy took a gulp of wine before continuing.

"She discovered that Winston had a gambling problem. Seems he might have owed a lot of money to some underground gambling people."

"Oh. Really?" Jack shoveled another forkful of lasagna in.

"Nans seems to think that might give him motive to kill Regis *now* instead of waiting for him to die." Lexy pushed the lasagna around on her plate. "Do you know anything about these poker games?"

Jack chewed, thinking carefully about his answer. "Well, you know organized gambling is illegal in this state, but that doesn't stop people from doing it. There a few gambling rings in the city. They move from place to place, so we can never bust them up. It's all hush-hush and, needless to say, attracts a nasty criminal element. If Winston was involved in those and owed them … well, let's just say he might be in dire need of money for sure."

"And do you think that would constitute motive?" Lexy asked while she cleared the dinner dishes and then broke out the pie.

Jack shrugged. "Hard to say. Where did Nans get this information, anyway? Is it reliable? And, for God's sake, please tell me she's not going to try to infiltrate the gambling ring."

Lexy grimaced as she sat down with her pie. "That's what I'm afraid of. An old friend that knows Winston told her and he seems to be pretty reliable. But you know how Nans is. She's apt to do something crazy, so I'm trying to get the information she needs before that happens."

"Smart idea." Jack pointed to the pie with his fork. "This is great pie."

"Thanks. You don't happen to have any contacts that could verify if Winston owed money, do you?" Lexy ventured.

Jack rubbed his hand through his short-cropped dark hair. "Lexy, you know I can't use police contacts for that stuff … even if I did have one, which unfortunately, I don't."

Lexy scooped up a forkful of whipped topping from her piece of pie and swirled it around in her mouth. "I don't suppose you have any idea where I could find out ..."

Jack shrugged. "I'm surprised Nans or one of the ladies doesn't have a contact. Heck, didn't Ruth date a gangster? Maybe they could ask one of Helen's old contacts at the paper. They usually have shady informants. Or maybe someone at the retirement center—thugs have grandmas, too, you know."

Lexy chuckled. "Let's hope she can dig some-one up. You know how she is—she won't rest until she finds out."

Jack nodded and then stood up and took the dishes to the sink. Lexy bent down toward Sprin-kles who had been patiently watching every bite that had gone into her mouth. She held out a tiny piece of pie crust.

"You want a treat?"

Sprinkles thumped her tail on the floor before gently taking the piece from Lexy and swallowing it in one gulp.

"So, are you ready to tackle some more pack-ing?" Jack put the last dish in the dishwasher.

Lexy's eyes slid to the back door—the one she used to use to cut through the back yards to

Jack's. "I guess we could finish up packing the rest of the kitchen cabinets."

"Yeah, I want to get those boxes to Goodwill this weekend." Jack led the way through the back door into Lexy's backyard, taking the shortcut through the missing board in the fence into his backyard.

"I guess we'll have to fix that fence before we list the house for sale," Jack said.

Lexy's heart tugged as she remembered the excitement of slipping through that hole in the fence on those early nights when she and Jack had first started dating. She had to admit, it had been pretty convenient to have her boyfriend right in the backyard. They'd been able to visit each other easily, and if one forgot their toothbrush ... well ... it was only a short walk to get it.

But now they were married and she got to have Jack at her house every night.

As she followed Jack to his kitchen door, a familiar beige car driving down the street caught her eye and she stopped in her tracks.

"Something wrong?" Jack stood at the back-door with the key in his hand.

"No." Lexy kept her eye on the beige car. It drove down Jack's street, then around the corner, then took a left onto Lexy's street.

Could it be coincidence that she had seen the car three times and now it was in her own neighborhood?

Lexy didn't think so.

Jack pushed the door open and started into the kitchen. Lexy held back, peeking throughout the bushes and neighbors' backyards, watching the car's progress. It stopped two houses down from hers on the opposite side of the street.

Almost as if it were staking out her house.

Lexy had a pretty good idea who was behind the wheel … and then she realized how she could kill two birds with one stone.

***

Lexy peeked into the kitchen. Jack stood at an open cabinet, digging out some coffee mugs. Cardboard boxes lay strewn on the floor. Old newspapers were stacked on the counters.

"I forgot my gloves at my house." Lexy wore latex food service gloves while packing to keep from getting all the newsprint on her hands. "I'll be back in a second."

"Okay," Jack shot over his shoulder as he started wrapping the mugs in newspaper.

Lexy tiptoed around to the front of Jack's house, then walked four houses down to the Murphy's. She turned into their yard, sneaking along the tree line and into the Sullivan's backyard. Hopefully neither the Murphy's nor the Sullivan's would look out the window and see her skulking around. The last thing she needed was for someone to call the cops on her.

Crossing from the Sullivan's backyard to their front, Lexy came out onto her own street, one house down from the beige car.

She ducked behind a rhododendron bush, then peered around it, ignoring the furry black and yellow bees that buzzed her. The driver of the car didn't notice her. He sat slouched in the driver's seat holding a pair of binoculars to his face. The binoculars were trained on Lexy's house.

She scurried across the street, ducked behind an azalea, then crab walked up to the passenger side of the car keeping her head below the windows, so the driver wouldn't be alerted to her approach.

When she reached the door, she grabbed the handle, then whipped the door open as fast as she could.

"Just what do you think you are doing!" she yelled. A startled Norman Shea whipped his head around to face her, his eyes bulging behind the coke bottle glasses.

"What ... I ... well ...," he stammered.

"You *do* realize my husband is a police detective." Lexy stood up, then bent down to look in the car at him. "I could have him arrest you *and* tell your mother about the toilet incident."

Norman blinked, then straightened in his seat. "The public deserves to know the truth."

"Yeah, but unfortunately, you're on the wrong trail." Lexy slipped into the passenger seat to Norman's obvious dismay. "However, I think I can help you get the truth and a juicy exclusive, too."

Norman eyed her suspiciously. "You're just trying to throw me off track."

"No. Listen. I've been looking into this with my grandmother."

Norman scrunched up his face. "Your grandmother?"

"Yes, perhaps you've heard of *The Ladies Detective Club*?"

"No."

"Well, that's my grandma and her friends. They're pretty good. They even help the police sometimes. Anyway, we've stumbled onto something much more interesting than a caterer serving the wrong ice cream."

That got his interest. "Really?"

"Yep. It seems Regis' death might not have just been an accident."

84

Norman's eyes got wider. "What do you mean?"

"His son, Winston, has some serious gambling debts. He needed money bad."

"But he already has lots of money."

"Not *this* much money. Even though he makes a big salary, Regis wasn't overly generous with the Bank's family fortune. The kind of debt Winston had is the kind that gets you maimed or killed. We're thinking maybe he couldn't wait for the old man to die and tried to help things along."

Norman speared her with a skeptical look. "How do you know this?"

"Let's just say we have our sources. But they need to be verified and that's where you come in."

"I do?"

"Sure, you must have some sources down at the paper that have street knowledge."

"Well, we do have some unsavory characters that I suppose I could tap into."

"Great, all you need to do is find out if Winston owed someone money and if he was being threatened."

"And then?"

"We'll do the rest to try to prove he killed Regis. And you'll get the exclusive on the story. No one else knows about this."

Norman chewed his bottom lip. "So, if I help you, you won't tell any other reporters and you'll keep me in the loop?"

Lexy nodded. "Yep."

"And you won't tell my mom about the toilets."

"Nope."

Lexy's stomach churned as Norman made up his mind. He tilted his head, then looked out the window and tapped his fingers on the steering wheel.

Finally, he shot out his hand toward Lexy for a handshake.

"Okay. Deal."

Chapter Nine

The next afternoon, Lexy sat at one of the cafe tables in her bakery, her hands wrapped around a mug of dark roast coffee. Across from her, Nans, Ruth, Ida and Helen munched on pastries. Outside, summer had arrived. The trees were in full bloom, flowers lined the river banks and birds hopped about on the sidewalk hoping for departing bakery customers to throw a few crumbs.

"These scones are delightful." Ida pinched off a piece of scone that contained a plump, juicy raspberry. "Are these the raspberries you got from the Farmer's Market?"

"Yes, they held up wonderfully and add a nice tart flavor, don't you think?" Lexy replied.

"They're great," Helen chimed in. "That Farmer's Market was nice ... I sure hope Larry doesn't end up getting screwed in Regis' will."

"I think he'll be fine. He didn't seem to care much about money," Ida replied.

"He sure doesn't spend it the way Winston does." Helen lifted the string of her tea bag, bobbing the bag up and down in her cup. "I was able to do some ... err ... *creative* investigation and it seems Winston and his wife have expensive tastes. Sure, he makes a lot at his vice president position in the company, but they spend more than his salary."

"So, if he did have a gambling problem, he'd be desperate for any money Regis left him," Nans said.

Ruth glanced around the shop, then leaned in, lowering her voice, even though they were alone. "Speaking of which, Shirley got a peek at the will. It turns out Winston is going to make out like a bandit ... even better than Larry and Olivia."

Lexy made a face. "Really? That hardly seems fair."

"I know," Ruth continued. "You see, most of the family money is in the form of *Banks Development* stock and Winston got a lot of stock—more than his brother and sister. I believe that was so he could retain the controlling interest in the company. Regis stipulated his direct issue be in control, so if any of them die within five years of Regis' death, their stock is split between the surviving siblings. Of course, there was some cash money, too, and they each got equal amounts of that right away."

"How much cash money?" Nans asked.

"One million each." Ruth's eyes sparkled.

"Well, that's enough to give any one of them motive to kill," Ida said.

"Maybe." Nans sipped her tea. "But the only one with an *immediate* need for the money was Winston. The others could have waited until Regis passed naturally."

"We aren't sure Winston had an immediate need, yet." Lexy glanced at her phone sitting on the table in front of her. *Where was Norman?* He was supposed to text her with whatever information he had dug up on Winston.

"I'm a bit worried, Lexy. How reliable *is* Norman?" Nans asked, as if reading her mind.

"He said he has some contacts from the paper that can get the information. That seems credible, doesn't it? I mean the paper would have reliable resources because they wouldn't want to print anything if they didn't have a pretty good idea it was true."

"Yes, the paper always did have some unsavory people they used for information, even in my day," Helen said. "But their information was usually spot on."

"Okay," Nans cuts in. "Say our theory is true and Winston did need the money. How can we prove he switched the ice cream?"

"Well, he *was* sitting next to him," Ida offered.

"It would have been easy to just slide his ice cream over and pull Regis's back in front of him, but we need something more concrete." Nans turned to Lexy. "Does that place have video cameras or anything?"

Lexy pressed her lips together. The lodge had been built decades ago. She doubted they had any type of surveillance. No one had mentioned it when she'd been there. "I doubt it."

"Too bad. If we had a video or pictures showing Winston switching the bowls, that would be just the proof we need!"

Pictures.

Lexy remembered someone from the Banks' family had hired a photographer to capture the event. "Wait a minute! What about the photographer?"

"That's right!" Nans snapped her fingers. "We need to get those pictures. Do you know who the photographer was?"

"No, but I could call Anna. I think she might know. She's been pretty frantic about all this harming her business and I wanna fill her in on the latest developments anyway."

"Good," Nans said. "What about eyewitnesses? It's a long shot there would be any pictures of the switch, so the next step would be to find someone who saw it happen."

"You served the head table, Lexy. Did you see anything?" Ruth asked.

Lexy took a deep breath and closed her eyes.

Had she seen anything?

She wracked her memory, but all she could remember was stressing over putting the right ice creams down and getting everyone served in time.

"No I was so busy serving, I wasn't watching the table. I was getting the evil eye from Regis' assistant. She was very stringent about the timing and we were running late."

"We'll have to talk to people that were there, find out who might have seen something. I didn't know most of them. Did you guys recognize anyone you know that we could ask?" Ida placed a scone in the middle of an unfolded napkin and then carefully tucked the edges around to cover it before shoving it into her purse.

"I didn't know anyone."

"Me, either."

"Didn't recognize a soul."

"That's going to make it difficult," Nans said. "People might not want to talk to strangers."

"I'm sure no one was watching the table that closely, anyway." Lexy got up to refill her coffee. "If someone saw the switch, wouldn't they have said something by now?"

"That's the thing," Helen answered. "They might not have noticed consciously … but something could be there in their subconscious."

91

Lexy stared at Helen, remembering the older woman was a master hypnotist. "You mean you want to hypnotize them?"

"Yep."

"That's an idea." Nans pushed some crumbs around on her plate. "It might be our only chance. But before we go to those lengths, I want to make damn sure we have a good reason to suspect Winston."

Lexy's phone chirped. She picked it up, her lips pressing together as she read the text from Norman.

"I think we might have a good reason. Word on the street is that Winston owed big gambling debts. Almost a million dollars. And from what Norman heard, some really nasty characters were itching to collect."

***

The rich aroma of freshly brewed coffee filled Nans' apartment. Lexy waited patiently by the old-fashioned stainless steel percolator, listening to the glugging noise and watching the coffee bubble up into the glass top of the cap.

A double-tiered tray of pastries sat on Nans mahogany dining room table. Plates had been passed out, napkins distributed and Nans' 1950s

Jadeite creamer and sugar set had been filled and placed in the middle of the table.

The whiteboard sat by the wall in the same place it had been before, except now it had more writing on it—the clues they'd found since the last time Lexy had been there.

"It's been fifteen minutes, Lexy. Any longer and the coffee will be too strong to drink!" Ruth yelled from her seat at the table.

Lexy liked her coffee strong, but took the hint and turned the percolator off. She poured coffees for everyone and handed them out before taking a seat.

"I've already hypnotized Mona, Ida and Ruth with no success," Helen said ruefully. "Hopefully, you girls will remember something."

"Have you ever been hypnotized before?" Ruth asked Anna.

"No." Anna looked around at them with wide, nervous eyes.

Lexy sympathized with her. She'd picked her up after work and filled her in on their theory. Anna had readily agreed to be hypnotized in the hopes she'd seen Winston make the switch. Anything to prove the liability wasn't with the catering.

"Oh, it's nothing," Lexy assured her with a sideways glance at Helen. Not that long ago, Helen had hypnotized Lexy. It had been painless—pleasant even—except for the strange side effect Helen had added in as a prank, which caused Lexy to quack like a duck whenever she drank coffee.

That had worn off now, but the four older ladies had gotten a big hoot out of it at the time. Lexy's eyes slid to her coffee mug. Hopefully, nothing like that would happen this time.

"Lexy, why don't you go first and Anna can see how it's done," Ida said.

"Okay." Lexy pulled her chair close to Helen who took Lexy's left wrist in one hand.

"Now, close your eyes and relax," Helen said in a low soothing tone. "You're safe here. You're on the beach, the waves coming in and out ... in and out. The sound of the surf, the gulls, the warming sun. The waves in and out ... in and out."

Lexy could feel herself relaxing, deeper and deeper. She settled back into the chair, not a care in the world.

"Picture yourself at Regis' birthday dinner," Helen droned. "You've just served the ice cream. What do you see?"

Lexy pictured the dining room at the lodge clearly in her mind's eye. "The room is all set up. Lots of people milling around."

"Can you see the head table?"

94

"Yes. The Banks family is seated with their ice cream."

"Focus on Regis ... what do you see?"

"He's sitting, talking to Winston, then leans over toward Olivia. Winston rips open one of those wet-naps and is rubbing his hands with it. Now Cora is behind them, bends down to whisper in Regis' ear. Oh, crap."

"What?"

"A man is approaching the table. Big, broad shoulders. Dark, longish hair, kind of curly. I don't know who he is, but he's blocked my view!"

Helen tightened her hold on Lexy's wrist. "Focus on the ice cream dish in front of Regis."

"That's the problem, I can't see it - my view is totally blocked! Wait. Now the man is moving away, going back to his table. Regis is standing up to make his speech. The ice cream could have already been switched and I didn't see it."

Helen sighed. "Okay, when I count to three you'll wake up refreshed and happy. One. Two. Three."

Lexy's eyes snapped open. She felt like she'd just slept the best sleep of her life. She remembered only bits and pieces about what happened while she'd been under hypnosis though. "Did you get anything?"

"Unfortunately, no. Someone blocked your view."

"Ughh ... Sorry. I'd hoped we'd be able to prove it was Winston. At least to ourselves, anyway. I don't think hypnosis is admissible in court, but at least *we'd* know and I'm sure Jack would believe us and open the case."

"Don't feel bad. All is not lost." Nans put the brownie she'd plucked from the top tier of the pastry dish on her plate. "Maybe Anna was watching from a different spot in the room and saw the switch."

Lexy got up and Anna sat in the chair next to Helen, who took her wrist and put her under hypnosis, the same as she'd done to Lexy.

"What do you see at the head table?" Helen asked.

"Cora. She's giving me a dirty look. She's unhappy we're late serving the ice cream."

"What about Regis. Can you see him?"

"Yes. He's talking to Winston ... now he's turned to listen to something Olivia is saying."

"Is he eating the ice cream?"

Anna paused. "No. It doesn't look like he's eaten any yet."

"Okay. What's happening now?"

"Someone at a table is signaling me. They want more coffee. I get a pot from the back and top off their cup."

"What about the head table?"

"Regis is making his speech."

Helen exchanged a look with Nans, who nodded. Lexy's stomach sank as Helen brought Anna out of the hypnotized state. Anna had been busy pouring coffee when the ice cream switch happened, so she didn't see the switch either.

"Well, that was disappointing." Ida mumbled, swooping the filling out of the side of a Whoopee pie with her finger and licking it off.

"I know," Nans sighed. "We'll just have to hope an incriminating shot shows up at the photographer's. A picture will be better anyway, as it will provide indisputable proof."

Ida turned to Anna. "Do you know who the photographer was?"

"Yes, Lexy asked me to bring his card." She fished a business card out of her back pocket and handed it to Ida who glanced at it and then passed it on to Nans.

Nans squinted at the card. "I'll get in touch with him first thing in the morning."

"Say, what was the big announcement Regis was going to make?" Helen asked.

Lexy and Anna looked at each other and shrugged. "No idea."

Ida wrinkled her brow. "That might be something. Maybe somebody didn't want him to make that announcement."

"Winston?" Ruth's brows lifted a fraction of an inch.

Ida shrugged. "Possibly, or maybe someone else."

"But why? And would it be something to kill over?" Helen asked.

"It's something to look into," Nans said. "I think we need to pay a visit to Regis' personal assistant. What was her name?"

"Cora," Anna said. "I don't know her last name, but she's still working for the Banks helping settle some of Regis' affairs."

"She could be a wealth of information," Ruth said.

"And she might know about the announcement," Helen added.

"It's settled, then. Tomorrow we'll call on Cora and the photographer." Nans turned to Lexy. "You better bake extra cookies tomorrow—there's nothing like fresh baked cookies to get people in a talkative mood."

Chapter Ten

The next morning passed in a flurry of baking. In between waiting on customers, Lexy and Cassie made extra batches of Snickerdoodles, chocolate chunk, peanut butter and, of course the old standby—chocolate chip cookies.

Lexy had packed two white bakery boxes full of the cookies and was ready to go when the ladies pulled up in front of *The Cup and Cake* in Ruth's giant blue Oldsmobile at eleven-thirty.

"Put your seat belt on." Ruth's eyes met Lexy's in the rear-view mirror as Lexy slid into the long backseat next to Nans. Lexy did as told and Ruth lurched the car away from the curb.

"So, what's the plan?" Lexy asked.

"Helen got a tip that Cora would be at Regis' office at noon. We're going to pay a visit to her there with the cookies to offer our condolences. We figure since you were the caterer, bringing some cookies to his office as a peace offering won't seem suspicious," Ida said from her spot in the front passenger seat.

Lexy squirmed in her seat. She didn't like being put on the spot.

"Oh, don't worry, I'll do all the talking," Nans said, as if reading her mind.

"After that we're heading straight to Elm Street to visit the photographer, Harry Wolf." Ruth added.

"That's right. He's on a photo shoot this morning, but said he'd be back to meet us at one o'clock. So we'd better get all our questioning in with Cora pretty quick," Nans said as Ruth pulled into *Banks Development* parking lot, swerving through the rows of cars before settling on a spot under a large oak tree in the back.

They piled out and walked to the one-story brick building.

"Gee, I was expecting something bigger," Lexy said. "A high-rise with lots of offices. I thought he had a big business."

"He does." Ida looked over the top of her large old-lady sunglasses at the building. "But he's not one to spend money on niceties. Plus, most of his workers are at the construction sites. This building is just for the management."

Nans held the door and they walked into a reception area with beige industrial carpeting and tan micro suede sofas. Several vases of flowers bloomed on various tables around the room. Condolence bouquets, Lexy assumed.

They approached a horseshoe-shaped faux wooden desk, behind which a young woman beamed a welcoming smile at them.

"Hi, we'd like to see Mr. Banks private assistant, Cora." Nans said in a brisk, business-like voice. "This is Lexy Baker who catered Mr. Banks birthday event and she has a condolence offering."

Lexy's stomach twisted as the girl's smile faltered. The receptionist frowned at Lexy. "I'm sorry, but she's not here—"

The door opened behind them. They all turn to see Cora, rushing in like she was in the world's biggest hurry. She stopped short, her flushed face registering surprise at the congregation in front of the desk.

"Looks like you're in luck," the receptionist said to Nans, then turned to Cora. "These people are here to give their condolences about Mr. Banks."

"Oh?" Cora scowled at Lexy. "Aren't you the caterer from Regis' birthday party?"

Lexy fought the urge to turn and run. Of course, running would have been impossible with the vise-like grip Nans had on her elbow.

"Yes. I'm the dessert caterer. I'm very sorry about the whole thing," Lexy squeaked out.

Cora looked sharply at Nans, Ruth, Ida and Helen. "And who are you?"

Nans introduced them and then held up the bakery box. "This is for the office. Lexy makes the best cookies."

Cora took the box, the frown still evident on her face.

"I wonder if we could have a moment of your time ..." Nans ventured.

"Me? What for? I'm very busy straightening out Mr. Banks projects for the hand-off."

"I'm sure you must be. But this is important." Nans leaned closer to Cora and lowered her voice. "It concerns Mr. Banks."

Cora stared at Nans skeptically, but something in Nans' tone must have piqued her curiosity. "Oh, all right then. Follow me."

Cora turned and walked toward a hallway. The women followed her. Lexy couldn't help but check out her shoes—her love of footwear drove her to it. She felt a pang of envy. Cora wore a pair of purple suede designer pumps with steel-tipped heels.

Cora stopped in front of an office suite and Lexy blurted out, "I love those shoes."

Cora glanced down, then frowned, bending to hurriedly wipe off a smudge on the tip of one of the shoes.

"Thanks, they're Manolo Blahnik," she shot over her shoulder continuing into the offices.

The outer office was plainly furnished with a desk, bookshelves and two filing cabinets.

This must be Cora's office, Lexy thought, looking at the clean surfaces. No messy papers or books. No signs of personal mementos either, except a small framed photo of a gnarled old oak tree against a sunset landscape on the windowsill. The office was neat as a pin, the only mess being a large amount of wet-nap packets all torn open and laying in the trash.

One wall had an impressive set of double doors that opened into a much grander, mahogany furnished office. The former office of Regis Banks was now filled with cardboard boxes. The bookshelves were half-empty. The filing cabinet drawers sat open, their contents in the midst of being transferred into cardboard storage.

Cora turned to them. "Now that Mr. Banks is gone, his son, Winston, will take this office. I'm just packing up the stuff Winston doesn't want."

"Will Winston keep you on?" Nans asked.

Cora shrugged. "I don't know what his plans are. We haven't discussed it."

"Do you even *want* to work for him? I heard he had some ... problems," Nans said.

Cora's sharp dark eyes assessed Nans. "Like what?"

"Oh, I don't know. Let's just say I hear he's not as good with money as his father."

Cora looked away. "Yes, that's true."

"You didn't notice any tension between Winston and Regis lately, did you?" Ruth cut in.

"Tension? You mean like as if they were fighting?" Cora worked at untying the pink string that Lexy had used to secure the bakery box.

"Yes. Maybe at the party ... or before it?"

Cora narrowed her eyes. Lexy thought she saw a ripple of emotion cross her face for a split second before she composed it into a stony mask. "Now that you mention it, Winston did seem rather nervous ... edgy."

"Any idea why?"

"No. I don't meddle in family business." She crossed to a row of cabinets and retrieved a large round platter, then came back to the desk and started to arrange the cookies on the platter.

"So, they weren't close?" Ruth asked.

Cora looked up from her cookie arranging. "Close? No, I wouldn't say so."

"But Regis left him in charge of the company," Nans pointed out.

"Yes, so it seems." Cora kept her attention focused on the cookies. "But I can't help but wonder if maybe Regis was having second thoughts."

Lexy felt her heart rate pick up speed. If Regis was having second thoughts about giving Winston the CEO role and all that stock, it would have given Winston another motive to get rid of him.

"Oh, really? Why do you say that? Did he mention something?" Nans asked.

"Not in so many words, but as you said, Winston wasn't as good with money and Regis knew that. He didn't want the company to flounder after he was gone. Of course, he expected to live many more years." She made a show of placing the last cookie on the platter. "Well, I shouldn't be talking out of school about that."

Nans' lips twitched. Lexy knew she wanted to press Cora about Regis changing his mind, but she must have thought better of it.

"What was that big announcement Regis was going to make at the party?" Nans asked.

Cora's face grew hard, her lips drawn into a thin line. "They're announcing development of a retail outlet mall over on the farmland on Meadow Road."

"Near the *Fur Fun K9 Center*?" Lexy asked. "That's such a beautiful piece of land. I didn't know it was being developed."

"Regis was trying to keep it under wraps."
"Oh, why?"

Cora sighed. "Some people in the community were opposed to it. Regis didn't want them to be able to muck up the works, so he was keeping everything mum until they were ready to start construction."

"Interesting." Ida raised her left brow. "But now with Regis gone, will Winston still develop it?"

"Yes," Cora said. "He's going to continue as planned. In fact, the announcement is coming out in today's paper."

Cora picked up the plate of cookies, balancing it in her left palm and then gestured toward the door with her right hand. "Well, if there's nothing else …."

They all took the hint and started out the door with Cora bringing up the rear. Just as she reached the threshold, Nans turned and looked back at Cora who had stopped a few paces behind her.

"One last thing. You don't think anyone would have switched the ice creams on purpose, do you?" Nans asked.

A look of shock took over Cora's perfectly composed features for a fraction of a second. The tray of cookies wavered slightly in her hand.

"Certainly not. What reason would someone have to kill an old man at his own birthday party?"

"Well, what do you make of that?" Ruth asked once they were in the car and on the way to Harry Wolf's.

"I get a vibe that she knows more than she's letting on," Nans replied.

"What about you, Ida?" Nans half-turned in the front seat to look at Ida. Her eyes went wide. "Ida, you didn't!"

Lexy peered around Helen in time to see a red-faced Ida shoving the last of a Snickerdoodle in her mouth.

"I only took *one*," she mumbled sheepishly, the words sounding distorted because of the cookie in her mouth.

"Oh, for crying out loud." Nans shook her head and clucked her tongue on the roof of her mouth. "So what did *you* think about our visit with Cora, Lexy?"

"She seemed distracted, but I guess I would be, too, if my boss just died and I was going to lose my job," Lexy replied.

Ida swallowed the cookie. "I'll tell you one thing, if Regis really was having seconds thoughts like Cora said, *that* would be a compelling motive for Winston to kill him sooner rather than later."

"And considering gangsters were pressuring him to come up with a large amount of money, that really ups the ante," Helen said.

"So, Winston looks pretty good for the crime," Ruth added.

"He sure does," Nans answered. "Plenty of motive."

"And what about the big announcement of that retail development on Meadow Road?" Helen asked.

Lexy's heart crunched. "I hate to see that. The area is so beautiful. I drive through it on the way to the *Fur Fun K9 Center* when I take Sprinkles to agility class. It's a shame to see it get turned into a strip mall."

"I bet the owner of the *Fur Fun K9 Center* feels the same way," Ruth said.

"You don't think that had something to do with Regis' death, do you?" Ida asked.

"No, Winston has a much more compelling motive. But I do think it would be a good idea to find out who opposed it and how adamant they were about it," Ruth replied. "People have killed over less before."

"I bet Norman can research some of that down at the paper for us." Lexy pulled out her phone. "I'll send him a text."

Nans glanced over at Ruth. "That theory doesn't wash with me, though. Someone switched the ice creams at his birthday party, and I doubt anyone who was in opposition to his big plans would have been invited."

Ruth pressed her lips together. "You have a point."

"Hey, isn't that the place?" Helen leaned into the front seat, pointing at a canopied storefront they were just passing.

Ruth jerked the car to the side of the road. The front wheel bumped up over the curb as the car squealed to a stop.

They piled out and proceeded to the shop, passing the candy store, *Oh Fudge!*, on the way. Lexy stopped for a mouthwatering second to gaze at the blocks of fudge in the window. She caught the eye of the store owner, Susan, and the two of them exchanged a wave.

"Are you coming?" Nans asked impatiently.

Lexy pulled herself away and hurried past the rest of the store fronts to *Wolf Photography*. Ruth was already at the door tugging on the handle, but the place was locked up tighter than a drum.

"I guess he's not here yet." Lexy shaded her eyes and looked down the street. A tall man in black jeans and tee-shirt rounded the corner. She recognized him as the photographer from the birthday party. Of course, it helped that he was carrying a camera and lugging photography gear.

"Here he comes," Ida stated the obvious.

He spotted them at the door and quickened his pace.

"Hi. You must be Mona. Sorry, I'm a little late." He glanced at Lexy. "Oh, yes, I remember you from the party. Sorry about your accident."

"Accident?" Lexy narrowed her eyes.

Harry frowned at her and Nans cut in. "She doesn't remember much, that's why it's so important we look at the pictures."

Lexy turned her narrowed eyes to Nans who brought her finger to her lips as Harry turned to open the door.

Lexy had no idea what Nans had told the photographer in order to get him to agree to show them the photos, but apparently it had something to do with her having an accident. Lexy shut her mouth and followed them inside—it was probably better that she didn't know.

Harry stopped short a few steps into the store, causing the ladies to pile into each other. Lexy peeked around them from the back, her heart sinking when she saw the state of the photography shop—it was in shambles.

"Someone's trashed the place," Ida said.

Harry's equipment case slid out of his hand to the floor. "Who would do this?"

He walked into the shop, a look of shock on his face. Drawers were pulled out, photographs on the floor, a mess everywhere.

"I'm so sorry," Nans said. "This is awful. Can we help you?"

Harry rubbed his hand through his curly hair, his eyes darting around the shop.

"Why don't you sit down?" Ruth pushed him into a chair. "Helen, get him some water."

Helen obeyed and Ruth opened the cookie box, "Eat this. The sugar will do you good."

"I'll call the cops." Nans pulled out her cell phone.

"Why would someone break in? Do you keep anything valuable in here?" Lexy asked.

"Just my cameras and equipment." Harry nodded toward a rack on the side that had an array of cameras and lenses. "But they're all still there."

"What about money?"

"No, I don't keep any here. Customers pay by credit card usually. Half down before the event and the other half after the pictures are ready."

Nans had wandered over to the counter where she eyed the messy piles of photographs, paperwork and supplies. Lexy noticed the supplies had been knocked over, dark piles of something wet and something powdery had spilled on the floor.

"Watch out, Nans. You don't want to step in that and mess up the crime scene," Lexy warned.

Nans stepped back, pointing to an area on the counter top where there was a square section void of the mess that sat on the rest of the counter. "It looks like something is supposed to be here."

"My computer!" Harry looked around the room. "It's gone!"

"Did you have sensitive data on it?" Lexy asked. "I hope you didn't lose something you can't recover."

Harry's shoulders sagged. "I might have. That's where I process all my digital photos. I unload them from the camera and manipulate them on the computer and then I make the prints and file them in that filing cabinet."

Lexy followed his gaze to a gray metal four-drawer filing cabinet that stood in the corner with the top drawer open. She walked over to it, looking in at the manila folders with clients' names listed alphabetically. The top drawer looked to hold A-G.

"Did you already file the pictures from the Banks birthday?" Lexy asked as she flipped through the tabs.

"Yes, there should be a folder in there."

Lexy looked through the tabs twice, then checked the other drawers. "I think I know what the thief wanted."

"What?" Nans asked. Everyone turned to look at Lexy.

"The pictures from Regis Banks' birthday party … the Banks folder is missing."

***

The police let Lexy and the gang leave after taking their names, addresses and phone numbers. They all piled into Ruth's Oldsmobile and she aimed it in the direction of Lexy's bakery. Lexy was in a hurry to get back to work. She still had a business to run and this case was taking up a lot of her time.

"Well, that clinches it," Nans said. "Someone switched those ice creams on purpose and wants to destroy any pictures."

"My money is on Winston," Ida said.

"Let's not be too hasty," Helen cut in. "That place was a mess. The folder could have been laying in one of those piles. We don't know for sure that whoever broke in took the Banks' folder."

"That's true," Lexy said. "We don't know for sure, but why else would someone break in? I'll have Jack keep us informed on the case."

"We'll have to see if we can track Winston's whereabouts this morning," Nans said. "Maybe your friend in the candy shop saw him ... or saw someone over at the photography place."

"Good thinking. I'll put a call into her." Lexy made a mental note to call Susan after work.

"If only we could search his place for the pictures ... or catch him disposing of them," Helen said.

Ida pushed forward in her seat, her eyes sparkling with excitement. "We might need to go on a stakeout."

"We could set up near his house tonight," Ruth offered.

"The car is pretty comfortable. It would be like an adventure and Lexy could bring some pastries and a thermos of coffee." Ida turned a hopeful face to Lexy.

"Sorry guys, but I'm taking Sprinkles to agility tonight."

"That's even better," Nans said. "You can pump your new friend, Olivia, for information on her brother."

"If we can just prove he has those photos, we could get this case tied up in no time. I'm sure

Jack would accept that as proof and arrest him," Ruth added. "Maybe Olivia knows where he was this morning or saw him with the pictures."

"I'll see what I can do," Lexy said, then looked at Nans with concern in her eyes. "In the meantime, you guys be careful. Olivia said Winston had a temper, and if he *is* the killer and sees you watching him, there's no telling what he might do."

Chapter Eleven

Lexy's heart tugged as she looked out the car window at the beautiful scenery on Meadow Road.

"Such a shame this is going to be a retail mall and parking lot soon," she said to Sprinkles who was busy looking out the passenger window.

Her thoughts turned to Nans and *The Ladies Detective Club*. Before leaving for the agility class, she'd packed them into Ruth's Oldsmobile with a thermos of coffee and a basket of pastries. She hoped they didn't get into trouble on their stakeout.

Sprinkles thumped her tail on the seat, anxious to get out as Lexy pulled into the *Fur Fun K9 Center*. She could barely wait for Lexy to open the passenger side door, wriggling through the small gap and leaping out before it was even all the way open.

The agility area was setup with a tall ramp and some hoops. Today's training involved running up and down the ramp and jumping through the hoops at various levels. Each activity had a command and Sprinkles was a fast learner and one of the faster and more agile dogs in the class—Lexy, not so much. Once again she felt winded at the end of the lesson, reminding her of how much she needed to get on track with her own exercise program.

After forty grueling minutes, the class broke up and Lexy headed out of the agility stadium. She could use a bottled water … but she had more important things to do. Like find out what was down that hallway in the back where she'd seen Olivia the other day. She had the distinct feeling something secretive was going on down there and with the news about the land development, it couldn't hurt to check it out.

"Come on, Sprinkles, let's do some detecting." She tugged Sprinkles down the hall, following the path she'd taken before. Luckily, her classmates had gone in the other direction and the halls were mostly empty, so there was no one to stop her.

She paused at the mouth of the hallway where she'd heard Olivia talking to the mystery man.

Should she venture down?

The building was old, probably a warehouse at one time, and the floors were some type of industrial tile. Luckily, she had sneakers on so she wouldn't make any noise. She took a deep breath and started down the dark wood paneled hall, the faint smell of baking dog food tickling her nose.

The back area of the *Fur Fun K9 Center* was like a maze, with hallways that led to other hallways all peppered with locked doors. Well, maybe they weren't all locked, but the few she'd quietly tried had been.

What was going on back here?

Lexy continued slowly down the hall, noticing that it intersected with a parallel hall about ten feet ahead. She was contemplating whether she should go right or left at the end when she heard voices coming from the left.

"… can't let anyone know … we're so close," a man's voice whispered.

"… if … finds out about the food, our efforts will have been wasted." Lexy recognized the upper crust twang of Olivia Banks' voice.

"Don't worry. I've taken care of that." The man again.

Lexy's heart kicked. They were coming her way! She realized she didn't have time to back down the hall without them seeing her, so she did the only thing she could think of.

"Sprinkles! No!" Lexy lunged back on the leash, jerking poor Sprinkles backwards just as the couple rounded the corner.

"Again?" Olivia looked at Lexy, her perfectly plucked brows forming a delicate 'V' on her forehead.

"What are you doing down here? These are our private offices," the man demanded, then he frowned at Olivia. "You know her?"

"Sorry, my dog ran off and I was just retrieving her." Lexy stuck her hand for the man to shake. "I'm Lexy Baker. My dog, Sprinkles, and I are taking the agility class."

The man eyed her dubiously before clasping her hand in his large calloused paw and giving it a firm handshake. "Steve Warren. I own the place."

"Nice to meet you," Lexy said.

Steve and Olivia continued down the hall, back the way Lexy had come. Lexy walked with them.

Lexy noticed that Olivia clutched a large green hardcover book to her chest—*The Book of Herbs.* "Nice to see you again. Where's your Pom?"

"Oh, Farfel? She's back there in the—" Olivia broke off, looking at Steve.

"Kennel," he completed for her.

"Oh, maybe that's what Sprinkles was after. She probably smelled dogs. Is there a boarding kennel back there or something?"

"Yes." Steve answered gruffly.

"What's with the herbs book?. Are you into herbs?" Lexy asked

Olivia's eyes darted over to Steve. "Yes ... I mean ... I have an herb garden as a hobby."

"Oh." Lexy wondered why she had the book *here*. "Are you interested, too, Steve?"

"Me?" Steve looked at her out of the corner of her eye.

"No, someone borrowed it from me and just returned it to me here," Olivia said before he could answer.

Lexy cleared her throat. "I just discovered they are planning on developing all the land around here. Some retail mall or something. It's too bad, the land is so pretty."

Steve's face turned hard. "Yeah, that's progress, I guess."

"It sounds like you're not a fan."

Steve shrugged. "I'm not. I like the open spaces, the fields and wildlife. A lot of animals will be displaced with the construction."

Lexy's heart melted a little. Maybe the guy was just a nature lover. "But I would think it would bring in a lot of extra traffic for the *K9 Center*," Lexy said.

Steve shrugged. "Maybe. But I like being out here in the country. It's more private."

"Well, it might be good for—".

Olivia's phone chirped, cutting off what she was about to say, but not before Lexy noticed Steve shoot her a warning glare.

What was that about? There was definitely something going on between them.

"Hello ... what?" Olivia frowned at the diamond-encrusted watch on her wrist. "Oh, is that today? I'll be right there."

She clicked off and shoved the phone in her Coach purse. "Sorry, I'm supposed to be at a hair appointment right now. I'm so bad with appointments—always mixing up the days. I have to run!"

Olivia clip-clopped away in a pair of purple suede Steve Madden wedges, leaving Lexy and Steve standing in the large entrance foyer.

"Well, I think you can find your way out, Ms. Baker." Steve nodded toward the left where the front door was. "Pleasure meeting you."

Lexy watched Steve walk away. He was tall and broad shouldered and the way he walked niggled something in Lexy's memory.

She was at her car before she remembered what it was. Steve Warren was the man that Lexy had remembered during hypnosis, the one who had blocked her view of Regis' ice cream.

***

Lexy's suspicions of Steve and Olivia were put to rest the next day when Nans called her at the bakery with news from their stakeout.

"We're on our way over with the proof to nail Winston!"

"What?" Lexy couldn't imagine what proof they had … had they found him with the pictures from the photography store? "From your stakeout?"

"You'll just have to wait and see." Nans hung up on her.

She hastily put together a plate of Snickerdoodles and Whoopee pies. She'd no sooner put the tray on one of the cafe tables when Ruth's car careened around the corner, grinding to a stop in front of the bakery. The four ladies jumped out, Nans with a pile of paper in her hand, Ida with a camera.

Nans ran into the bakery, waving the papers.

"Look at these." She spread them out on the table.

Thankfully, no customers were in the bakery and Lexy could focus on the pictures. She looked down at them, her heart pumping with excitement as she went through the series. Winston at a park with a large briefcase, then him handing it to a man, then the two men moving away from each other in different directions.

"Those are just some still photos we printed off from this video." Ida shoved the camera in front of Lexy's face. She watched as Winston gave the briefcase to the man, then walked away.

"I can't wait to show this to Jack." Nans green eyes sparkled. "Let's FaceTime him with your iPhone."

Lexy pressed her lips together. The photos *did* seem suspicious, but what did they prove? Jack didn't like being summoned to talk on FaceTime unless it was critical.

"I'm not sure this is enough evidence to prove Winston was the killer. All it shows is him handing over a briefcase. We don't even know what's in it," Lexy said.

"Why, that thing's obviously loaded with money. Just look at who he's handing it to." Ida jabbed her index finger toward the face of the other man in the photo.

Lexy squinted at it. "Who?"

Ida gave an exasperated sigh. "Don't you recognize him? That's the notorious gangster Clubs McGinty ... tell her, Ruth."

"Yep, that's Clubs. I knew him quite well when I hung around with Nunzio." Ruth ducked her head sheepishly. "He runs most of the illegal gambling around here."

Lexy's eyebrows rose at the mention of Nunzio Bartolli. Ruth had had a fling with the retired mobster and almost been arrested for his murder a while back. Lexy and *The Ladies Detective Club* had to pull out all the stops to find the real killer and get to the bottom of why Nunzio was murdered.

"Clearly, there's only one reason why Winston would be handing Clubs that briefcase," Nans tapped her iPhone impatiently.

"Okay, I'll FaceTime Jack, but he's probably going to be mad at me for doing so." Lexy pulled out her iPhone and clicked the FaceTime app, then pressed Jack's id, chewing her lip nervously as it rang.

"Lexy, what's going on? Is something wrong?" Jack's concerned face filled her phone screen.

"No. I have Nans here. She has something important for you." Lexy handed the phone over to Nans like it was a hot potato.

"Hi, Jack!" Nans yelled into the phone.

"Mona, what's going on?" Jacks face turned from concerned to amused.

"I have some important evidence for you in the Regis Banks case."

"Case? There's no case. We determined it was an accidental death due to his food allergy."

"Oh, I know, but once you hear what we've found, I think you'll change your mind."

Jack's heavy sigh blared out from the phone. "Okay. But be quick. I have a call to go on."

"We found out that a member of his family has some gambling trouble. Big trouble. And they needed money to get out of that trouble. Money that they'd get when Regis died."

"That's not enough to prove he was murdered."

Nans continued on, "This person switched ice creams at the birthday party. We think the switch might have been captured by the photographer, Harry Wolf. Tell me, did you find the Banks folder in Harry Wolf's studio?"

"No," Jack's face took on a more interested look. "It never turned up."

"I thought so."

"That's still not enough to prove murder," Jack said.

"No, but this might be." Nans pointed the iPhone screen at the pictures laid out on the table so Jack could see them. "That's the killer right there, meeting with Clubs McGinty and handing over a large briefcase, presumably filled with money. Money he got from killing his own father."

"Those pictures are hard to see … who is that?"

"Winston Banks," Nans announced. "Are you going to arrest him?"

Another sigh from the phone. "I'm afraid I can't."

"Nans scrunched up her face and whipped the iPhone back to face her. "Why the heck not?"

"Because Winston Banks was found dead less than an hour ago."

Chapter Twelve

"Heart attack, my patootie," Nans said after Jack explained what he knew about Winston's death. They'd called for him to come on the scene only because Winston had died at the office, but all evidence indicated he'd had a heart attack.

"It sure sounds like one," Lexy replied. "Jack said the people that were in the meeting with him reported that he complained about a tingling and numbness in his arm, then he slumped over. He died before the ambulance arrived."

Nans narrowed her eyes at Lexy. "Doesn't it seem rather odd to you that two members of the same family die within the same week?"

"Yeah, but we thought *Winston* was the killer."

"I know." Nans tapped her finger on her lips. "It sure did seem like he was. I guess our investigation got thrown off track."

"His death does complicate things." Ida peered into the pastry case. "Lexy, can you get me a Whoopie pie?"

"Do you think the same person killed both of them?" Helen asked Nans as Lexy moved behind the pastry case. "Oh, and I'll have a Snickerdoodle while you are back there."

"Of course. It has to be the same person," Nans replied to Helen, then turned to Lexy at the bakery case. "Put me in for a Snickerdoodle, too."

"Winston could have killed Regis and died of a heart attack. He was under a lot of stress what with being a murderer and owing money to gangsters," Lexy pointed out as she piled pastries onto a tray.

"I'll take a brownie if you don't mind," Ruth chimed in and Lexy added a brownie to the tray.

Nans pulled out chair and slumped into it. "He *could* have died naturally, but my instincts tell me he didn't."

Ruth, Ida and Helen nodded their agreement and joined Nans at the table. When it came to murder, Nans' instincts were almost always right on the button.

"But he died in the middle of a meeting with witnesses and the EMT's said it looked like it was his heart," Lexy said. She put the pastries on the table and then moved over to the coffee center to pour coffees. "Surely someone would have seen something if anyone in the meeting killed him."

"Maybe not," Ida cut in, "if he was poisoned before the meeting. Maybe someone put something in his coffee or the food they served."

"I hope Jack's thought of that," Nans said. "We should call him and make sure he tests anything Winston ingested."

"But he already said they don't suspect foul play."

"Better to be safe than sorry." Nans picked up her phone. "I'll just text him."

"There is another explanation, too." Ruth offered. "Maybe there are two killers. Winston killed Regis and then someone else killed Winston."

"Who would want to kill Winston?" Lexy brought the coffees to the table and passed them out, then took a seat herself. "He'd already paid off his gambling debt, so it wasn't the gangsters. Plus, they'd use a more direct method, I assume."

Ruth nodded. "Yeah, it wasn't Clubs McGinty. He'd use guns."

Nans stood and paced back and forth in front of the table. "We know that Winston was going to carry on with the development project. That's what he and Regis have in common. Maybe it was someone who wants that project stopped."

"It could be," Helen said. "Who will be in charge of the company now that Winston is gone?"

Everyone looked at each other in silence.

"We need to find that out," Nans said. "We already know there are plenty of people who didn't want the development. Wasn't Norman getting us a list of people who opposed it?"

Lexy nodded. "I'll text him and see if he has that yet."

"This is getting stranger and stranger." Ida bit into her Whoopee pie. A dollop of cream squirted out the side and she licked it away. "If Regis and Winston were killed for the same reason, it has to do with the company ... or the family money."

"Or maybe it has nothing to do with either," Helen shrugged. "We went down the wrong trail before."

"It bears looking into, but you know what the number one rule is when investigating a murder." Nans bit into her Snickerdoodle.

"Follow the money," Ida, Ruth, Helen and Lexy chorused.

"And who would have benefitted financially from Winston's death?" Ida asked.

"It's usually the spouse," Nans replied. "But, since we don't know what's in Winston's will, we can't say for sure."

"That's right, Winston's widow, Evelyn." Ruth sipped her coffee. "If he was poisoned, she'd have had access to him before he went to the office. She might have done it then, or put it in a bagged lunch. Some of those poisons have a delayed effect."

"She was also at the birthday party and could have switched ice creams," Helen added.

"And we already know she didn't share a lot of Winston's views." Lexy thought back to their meeting at the Farmer's market.

"But, what motive would she have to kill Regis?" Ida asked.

"That's easy. Winston inherited a lot of money and stock from Regis. If Evelyn is his beneficiary, now all that goes to her."

"If that's the case, she had a very clever plan." Nans spread a napkin out on the table and piled two Snickerdoodles inside it, folded the edges over the cookies and stuck it in her purse.

"And almost got away with it," Ruth added, "by making the deaths look like either accidental or natural."

"We don't know for sure that Winston's death *wasn't* natural," Lexy reminded them. "Besides, Evelyn doesn't seem like the killer type. She seemed like a nice, caring person when we saw her at the Farmer's Market. I can't picture her killing two people for money."

Nans gave Lexy a look. "That's the thing about killers that almost get away with it—they're always the ones you suspect the least."

Chapter Thirteen

Lexy kept herself busy the rest of the day with baking and waiting on customers. Sometime in between frosting chocolate brownies and filling cream puffs, Anna had called wanting to know about the case and to have Lexy look over an invoice from the Banks' birthday party. Since Lexy was already planning to stop at Nans' that evening to go over the clues, she arranged for Anna to meet her there.

Anna's catering van was already parked in the back of the lot when Lexy arrived at the retirement center.

Anna jumped out of the van with some papers in her hand. "Hey, Lexy! How is it going?"

"Great. How about you? Has your catering business suffered at all because of the … ummm … incident?" Lexy grimaced.

"No. Thankfully, nothing got in the press, so I don't think any customers have been scared off. But I heard about Winston Banks and I'm a bit worried. I thought you guys said he was the killer."

"We *thought* he was," Lexy said. She started toward the entrance, balancing the coffee cake she'd brought in one hand. Anna fell in step next to her. "We actually have pictures of him handing over the money he owed. But just because he's dead, doesn't prove he wasn't the killer."

Anna scrunched her face up. "True, but it does add a strange twist, doesn't it?"

"It sure does." Lexy opened the glass door and the two navigated the halls to Nan's apartment.

"I brought this invoice from the Banks' birthday party. I've had a heck of a time getting Cora to pay me. But I guess rich people like to hold on to their money for as long as they can."

Lexy laughed. "That's for sure. That's how they stay rich."

"Anyway, I was hoping you could look it over and make sure I have the bakery prices correct."

"No problem. We'll do that first thing and then we can discuss the plan of action with Nans and the ladies."

Lexy's fist tapped on Nans' door, which opened immediately.

"We've been waiting for you." Nans pulled her inside where Ida was ready to relieve her of the bakery box.

Ida smiled as she peered inside the box. "Oh, I love coffeecake."

Ruth and Helen were already seated at the table. The whiteboard sat in its usual place against the wall. Lexy could see the ladies had been busy updating it with new information.

Nans got coffees for Anna and Lexy and they all sat down at the table. Anna slid the invoice over to Lexy. "Let's just get this out of the way."

Lexy looked down the list of items, squeezing her eyes shut and mentally comparing the list to what she'd delivered at the party.

"Looks good." She hovered a pen over the bottom of the invoice where she could see Cora's signature of two scrawls with a large C and S at the beginning of each scrawl. "Should I sign under Cora?"

"If you just initial it that will be fine," Anna said.

Nans pushed her chair out and stood at the whiteboard. "If you ladies are done we can get on with it."

Lexy and Anna nodded and everyone turned their attention to Nans.

"Okay, then, let's recap. Since Winston's death we've been looking at other suspects. His wife Evelyn is high on our list because she would gain the most financially and also because she didn't agree with the company business. But since Regis' had the stipulation in his will that all stock be kept amongst his children, she won't get any of Winston's stock and won't gain a controlling interest in the company."

Anna's eyes widened. "But how do you think she killed him? The paper said he died of a heart attack."

"We figure she probably used some sort of poison. She could have put it in his breakfast, or maybe she gave him a bagged lunch or something. Some toxins don't take effect right away. He died in an early morning meeting at work, so he was most likely poisoned there or shortly after he left home."

"Using poison is a similar method to how Regis died. He died from his food allergy. These types of methods are preferred by women because they are not messy or bloody," Ruth chimed in.

"Do you think she killed Regis, too?" Anna asked.

"She may be a very clever killer." Nans tapped something on the whiteboard under the 'Motive' category. "She may have planned it out from the beginning. Kill off Regis first so Winston inherits the money, then kill Winston and get it all for herself."

"I did notice at the birthday party that she and Winston didn't seem to get along," Lexy said.

"Gosh, I don't think it could be her." Anna shook her head. "I talked to her quite a bit when planning the party and she was very nice. A kind and loving person. She didn't seem to care very much about money. I can't picture that she planned this whole thing out in cold blood just for financial gain."

Nans smiled. "Like I told Lexy, those are the ones you have to watch out for."

"So what's the plan?" Ruth spread her arms looking at Nans. "How do we prove she's the killer?"

"We need to catch her at something." Nans picked her coffee up from the table and sipped. "If she is the killer, she has something to hide. Maybe the poison she used for Winston … or the photos from the party."

"And she'll need to dispose of that incriminating evidence," Ida added.

"And the best way to catch her doing that is to have her under surveillance," Nans said.

"But not in Ruth's car." Helen paused her forkful of coffee cake halfway to her mouth. "That big old boat stands out too much and we almost got caught when we tailed Winston. We need a much smaller, less obvious car."

Everyone turned to look at Lexy, and her stomach did a nervous somersault.

"Oh, no, not me. Jack wouldn't like that. Plus, I have too much work to catch up on to go around tailing suspects. But I think I know someone who would love to help." Lexy pulled out her phone and dialed Norman.

"Hey, Norman, how would you like to help us stake-out Winston's killer?"

"Winston's killer?" Norman's voice was hushed. "Word around here is he died of a heart attack … although I do admit I had my suspicions when I heard it."

"We're suspicious, too. Nans wants to do a stake-out on our prime suspect to see if she can pick up any evidence, but they don't want to use Ruth's car. It's too noticeable. Are you game to use yours?"

"Sure, that would be great. I'd love to see how your grandmother and her friends operate. I could learn a lot from them."

Lexy frowned. "Really?"

"Of course. Oh, and I got that information you guys wanted … about the people who opposed developing the land on Meadow Lane. Turns out a lot of people opposed it, not the least of which is Steve Warren who owns the *Fur Fun K9 Center*."

"Oh, really?" Lexy's brows lifted. "That's interesting."

"And I found out something else, too." Norman's voice was laced with excitement. Lexy could picture him huddled over his phone, whispering into it. "It seems there was a big controversy about that land way back when *Banks Development* bought it. Regis practically stole the land from the Silversteen's, using all kinds of dirty tricks on the poor elderly farmer and his wife.

"The land had been in the family for generations. The farmer came on hard times and Banks took advantage through some shady loan. Practically threw the couple and the granddaughter they were raising out on the street. He made a big stink in the press, but nothing could be done since Regis never actually did anything illegal."

"That sounds like him," Lexy said, "I bet there's plenty more stories like that."

"I'll keep digging," Norman said. "And I'll bring the list of the opposers tonight. What time should we meet?"

"I won't be going, but you can come over to the retirement center tonight at ..." Lexy eyed Nans.

"Seven o'clock." Nans said. "Tell him we'll pack some sandwiches and snacks to keep us fortified."

Lexy relayed the information to Norman, then disconnected.

"Now if we only had an inside track to Winston's autopsy results," Helen glanced sideways at Lexy. "Maybe you could call Jack?"

"You know Jack doesn't like to talk about cases to me," Lexy said, then sighed at the puppy dog faces Nans, Ruth, Ida and Helen gave her. "All right, but I'm not going to press him."

Lexy still had her phone in her hand, so she tapped in Jack's number and waited for him to answer.

"Hi, Lexy." Jack's voice sounded relaxed, which was good. Not only did she hate to bother him when he was busy, but she could never get any good information out of him when he was trying to rush off the phone.

"Hi Hun. I'm here with Nans and the gang and we were wondering about Winston Banks."

"Anything specifically?" Jack's voice was guarded.

"Did you have an autopsy done?"

"Yes, as a matter of fact we did."

Lexy's pulse picked up a notch with excitement. Nans came over next to her and Lexy held the phone out from her ear so Nans could listen in. "Did you find anything unusual?"

"Well, not per se," Jack said. "On the surface it looks like he had a heart attack."

"But ..." Lexy let the word hang. She could tell Jack had his doubts. She just hoped he'd voice them.

142

"It's just that something doesn't sit right. I mean, with him dying so close to his father and Winston didn't have any history of heart disease."

Nans leaned closer and yelled into the phone. "Jack, it's Mona."

"Hi, Mona. I figured you'd get on the line sooner or later."

"Listen, I think it might be in your best interest to do a broad toxicology test. Not the standard one that's typically done. I have a theory."

"Sure, Mona, I'm sure the medical examiner won't mind doing that, especially when I tell him my wife's grandmother has a theory," Jack said with good natured sarcasm. He didn't like it when Lexy and Nans tried to investigate on their own, but the truth was he had a lot of respect for Nans' detecting skills and had even asked the ladies to consult on certain cases.

"Just tell him I'll bring him one of my apple pies," Nans said.

Jack laughed. "I'll see what I can do. I gotta run—see you at home tonight, Lexy."

"Apple pie?" Lexy asked Nans as she put down the phone.

Nans smiled, "Mike, the medical examiner, loves my pies."

"Those pies sure do come in handy as bribes," Ida said.

"I'm not above throwing out an apple pie bribe to further the case." Nans went to the whiteboard and updated it with the new information.

"Well, it does sound like Jack has doubts and you know his instincts are spot on," Ruth broke off a piece of coffee cake and stuffed it in her mouth.

"Just in case he's not, there's another suspect I think we should look at," Lexy said.

"Who?" Nans wrinkled her brow at Lexy.

"Olivia."

Lexy told them about her conversation with Olivia and Steve at the *K9 Center*. "They were acting strange—evasive. I know they are hiding something and Steve was one of the big opposers to the land development out there."

"But, what would Olivia have to gain from killing both Regis *and* Winston?" Helen asked.

"I don't know, but in the conversation I overheard, they seemed afraid someone "might find out about the food" and Steve said he'd take care of it." Lexy chewed her bottom lip. "Maybe they killed Regis and Winston was onto them, so they killed Winston to keep him quiet."

"How would they have had access to poison Winston?" Helen asked.

"We're not sure he *was* poisoned," Ruth said.

Helen rolled her eyes. "Right, but either way they would have had to have access to him in order to kill him."

"He was Olivia's brother. Maybe they met before the meeting. Maybe Olivia was at the office," Lexy suggested. "The other thing is that I recognized Steve … or his back, anyway. He was the person that blocked my view from the ice creams at the birthday party."

"You mean the one you saw under hypnosis?" Helen asked.

Lexy nodded. "He was up at the head table and Olivia was sitting right next to Regis, so either one of them could have switched the ice cream."

"One of them could have created a diversion and the other switched them!" Ruth said.

"What was he doing at Regis birthday party if he opposed the development?" Ida asked. "I would think they would be opponents of sorts."

"True, but Olivia and he are tight, so she probably invited him," Lexy said.

Nans scribbled a note about Olivia and Steve on the board. "It doesn't hurt to cover all the angles. Will you be able to check into that further, Lexy?"

"Yes, in fact, there's an agility event tonight that will give me the perfect excuse to snoop around." Lexy looked at her watch. "But I better get going if I want to get there on time."

"Great, so it's settled," Nans said. "We'll stake out Evelyn and Lexy will dig into Olivia and Steve's secret. We'll meet back here tomorrow at oh-nine-hundred sharp."

"Perfect." Lexy pushed herself away from the table.

"I'll walk out with you," Anna offered.

The two girls were almost out in the hall when Nans called after them.

"Oh, and Lexy … don't forget to bring plenty of pastries when we meet tomorrow morning."

Chapter Fourteen

Lexy headed home after she left Nans, her hopes of catching up on some work at the bakery fading when she realized it was already six o'clock. She barely had time to collect Sprinkles and rush off to the *Fur Fun K9 Center* for the agility event.

They pulled into the car-jammed parking lot at six-thirty, about an hour before sunset. The grounds were alive with activity. Lexy got out of the car hesitantly. The crowded event would provide her the perfect opportunity to snoop around—she just hoped she wouldn't get caught.

Sprinkles didn't feel nearly as hesitant as Lexy. She bounded out of the car, straining at the leash to explore the smells and sights of the event.

Lexy reined Sprinkles in and made her way into the crowd. The warm blanket of early summer evening air was perfumed with lilacs from the twelve foot tall old hedges at the edge of the parking lot. Lexy wondered if the lilacs were on the *K9 Center* property, or if they'd be ripped up with the retail development.

The main agility event was inside with different dog classes competing in groups. The resting groups usually retired to wait it out in their cars and many of the cars in the parking lot had their hatches open, owners sitting on the edge of the lift gate eating sandwiches, their dogs inside crates or sitting happily beside them. On the tail-gates were the tools of dog competition—water bowls, brushes, combs and dog toys. It was the canine version of a tail-gate party.

Lexy passed a few of her agility classmates and nodded a quick greeting. She didn't have time to stop to talk—she had work to do.

She skirted past the edge of the parking lot to the side of the building. Various vendors were set up down the length of the building all the way to the back. They were selling anything from dog bowl sets to ice cream to dog food. The smell of fried sausage, peppers and onions made Lexy's mouth water. She'd forgotten to eat supper.

As she strolled past the booths, she wondered if she should set up a bakery stand at the next event. By the way people were lined up at the sausage cart and ice-cream stand, there were plenty of hungry people.

But then she came to the end of the row and her mind turned to more important matters. If her calculations were correct, the locked rooms in the corridor in back of the *K9 Center* would be against the wall at the back of the building here. If she was lucky, they might even have doors that led outside. And if she was even luckier, she might be able to listen in at one of those doors and find out what was really going on back there.

Glancing back over her shoulder to make sure she wasn't being watched, Lexy slipped around the corner of the building out of sight of the crowds.

Sprinkles was just as happy to sniff the ground in the back of the building as she was in the front and she happily walked along beside Lexy as they skirted along the edge. In the back, the building was 'U' shaped, the ground mostly dirt with patches of dry grass. Two large dumpsters sat in the middle of the 'U'. The approaching sunset cast the back of the building in shadows. Lexy hoped that would make her less visible if anyone came outside.

There were four doors in the back of the building. Lexy stood staring at them, trying to decide which one to sidle up to. Sprinkles made the decision for her, pulling her toward the door to the far right.

As they got closer, Lexy could hear Sprinkles making loud sniffing noises, her nose twitching madly. Lexy could smell something, too—it smelled like baking, but not sweet pastry—more like crackers or—dog food.

Did the K9 center make its own dog food?

She didn't think so. She was sure someone would have mentioned it to her by now. But if they didn't, then what were they baking behind that door?

Lexy got closer, pressing her ear to the edge. She could hear voices and other sounds. Someone was in there, but the noise was muffled by the door and she couldn't make out what they were saying.

"Darn it, Sprinkles. I can't hear a thing. What do you think is going on in there?"

Sprinkles looked up at her, raising one of her white brows, then lifted her nose in the air and pointed it at the dumpster, pulling Lexy over and sniffing the whole way.

The dumpster had less pleasant smells. Sour milk. Rotting garbage. Lexy's stomach churned. She was about to tug Sprinkles away when she heard the door open behind her. Her heart kicked and she scurried to the other side of the dumpster, squatting down and praying she hadn't been spotted.

"Make sure you set the special packages aside," a man's voice said. "We don't want them going in with the regular dog food."

150

Lexy heard the scuff of feet on the dry dirt coming closer to the dumpster. She held her breath, her heart racing as she wiped sweaty palms on her jeans. She eyed Sprinkles anxiously. The last thing she needed was for the dog to bark or make any noise that would cause them to be discovered. Sprinkles sat quietly beside her, but Lexy's mind raced for a plausible explanation just in case.

"Of course. The special stuff is going directly to Michael, right?" Another man, deeper voice.

Lexy cringed at the hollow clang of something heavy being heaved into the dumpster.

"Yep, he's coming later on with the money and—" the first man's words sounding farther away and then cut off as the door closed.

Lexy took a deep breath and let it out slowly. This wasn't the first time she had been forced to hide behind a dumpster. You'd think she might be getting used to it by now, but it was still nerve wracking. Still, it *was* much better than having to get *in* the dumpster to search for a murder weapon—something she'd also had to do before.

After a few minutes of silence, Lexy figured it was safe to come out. She stood on her tip toes, peeking into the dumpster to see what they'd thrown in. Nothing but cardboard, old food and what looked like chopped up leaf stems on the top. They must have thrown in the cardboard and stems.

What would they be doing with leaf stems?

Lexy stared at the closed door the men had come through, replaying the conversation in her mind.

Special dog food?

Michael coming with the money?

Lexy knew Steve and Olivia were trying to hide something, and in the previous conversation she'd overheard, they'd mentioned food. Could they be mixed up in some shenanigans that had to do with dog food?

Lexy backed toward the edge of the building, pulling Sprinkles along with her.

What could possibly be going on with the dog food that would be worth killing over?

Lexy rounded the corner of the building and headed back out into the commotion of the crowd. She'd missed supper, so she gave in and bought a sausage, pepper and onion sub, then brought it to her car where she sat on the hood to eat it.

She savored the juicy sandwich, swiping at the grease on her lips with the tiny inadequate napkin the vendor had provided. Sprinkles danced around the front of the car, her eyes brimming with hope that a morsel of food would fall from the sub.

Lexy tossed her a piece of sausage, careful not to include any onions. She knew they weren't good for dogs.

Her mind went back to what she'd heard by the dumpster. The man had said something about special packages that he didn't want mixed in with the regular dog food. That implied the packages *looked* like dog food, but had something 'special' in them.

Something that someone named Michael would pay money for.

Were Olivia and Steve mixed up in smuggling drugs disguised as packages of dog food?

Chapter Fifteen

The next morning, Lexy got to the bakery early and finished most of the day's baking by the time Cassie came in. She left Cassie in charge and brought scones to Nans, arriving at nine a.m. sharp as instructed.

Lexy hummed with excitement over her discovery by the dumpster the night before as she knocked on Nans' door.

Nans whipped the door open, her bright eyes dancing. Lexy knew that look—apparently, Nans had a discovery of her own.

"Come in, dear. We have something very interesting to show you."

Inside, Ruth, Helen and Norman were hunched over a series of photographs that were laid out on top of the dining room table.

"Hi, Lexy," the three of them muttered without even looking up at her.

Ida came over and relieved her of the pastry box, then got to work setting the scones on a platter. Over in the kitchen, the percolator bubbled. Lexy followed the smell of fresh brewed coffee, grabbed a mug from Nans' cabinet and stood in front of the machine.

Nans dragged Lexy from the kitchen before she could fill her mug. "Look what we discovered on our stakeout!"

Nans gestured toward the pictures. Lexy squinted at them, leaning closer to the table. The pictures were blurry, like they were taken with the shaky hand of an eighty year-old. Which, Lexy figured, they had been.

In the first two pictures, she could make out a couple in a romantic embrace. In the third, they step away from each other. The fourth was a close-up of their heads.

Lexy sucked in a breath. "Is that Larry and Evelyn?"

"You bet your sweet bippie," Ida said around a mouthful of scone.

Lexy stared at the ladies with wide eyes. "You mean they were having an affair?"

"Looks like it." Helen headed toward the coffee urn, taking Lexy's mug on the way over.

"Isn't that wonderful?" Ruth asked. "That gives them three reasons to kill Winston!"

"Three?" Lexy's brows dipped at Ruth.

"Yep." Nans walked to the whiteboard, then pointed at a list under the heading 'Motive'. "To get the money, to stop the development, and to be together."

"And don't forget." Helen came back to the table from the kitchen, handing Lexy a mug full of steaming black coffee. "Cora said she thought Regis was going to cut Winston out of the will, so that would create an immediate need for them to get rid of Regis before he cut Winston out. Otherwise, they wouldn't benefit from the money Winston inherited."

Lexy looked back at the pictures. "These don't prove they were having an affair ... just that they were embracing."

"True, but it shows they are *very* fond of each other," Nans said.

"More than a brother-in-law and sister-in-law should be." Ida wiggled her eyebrows.

"Well, I can't say I'd blame Evelyn. Olivia said she suffered the brunt of Winston's temper and I thought I saw a bruise on her arm when we saw her at the Farmer's Market. Winston might have been hitting her," Lexy said.

"Yet another motive for her to kill him," Helen added.

Lexy's shoulders slumped. "Well, that trumps my discovery."

"What did you discover?" Nans asked.

Lexy told them about the conversation she'd heard by the dumpster and the stems she'd seen inside it.

"Stems?" Ruth scrunched her face up. "The only drug I know in which stems are used is marijuana and I doubt they'd be smuggling that … it's too readily available."

"It is?" Lexy narrowed her eyes at Ruth, wondering exactly how she knew *that*.

"Of course. Why, you can even get it here at the retirement center."

"For medicinal use only," Nans said sharply.

"Anyway, I'm not sure what the stems would be for," Ruth continued. "Maybe they're doing something with vegetables or herbs."

Lexy remembered Olivia had that book on herbs the last time she saw her. "Hmmm … maybe. But there *is* something suspicious going on, for sure. I mean, why would this mysterious Michael person be coming to hand over money?"

"That is a good question. But my money is on Larry and Evelyn." Ida tapped the picture of the kissing couple with her index finger.

"If Olivia and Steve are smuggling drugs in dog food, why would they have to kill Regis and Winston?" Helen asked.

Lexy pressed her lips together. "I'm not sure. They might feel that developing that land right next to the *Fur Fun K9 Center* would turn a lot of eyes on the operation and they'd be discovered."

"Or maybe Winston or Regis discovered their operation already," Ruth added.

"I'm not so sure about Olivia. Evelyn and Larry both had plenty of access to poison Winston *and* Regis," Norman, who had been watching the old ladies like a groupie at a rock concert, piped up.

"I can't believe it could be them, though … they seem so nice!" Lexy said.

Lexy's phone chirped. She dug it out and looked at the display. Hope bloomed in her chest when she saw who it was.

"It's Susan from the fudge shop. Maybe she saw Larry or Evelyn there the morning the birthday party photos were stolen," Lexy said. "That will give us another piece of evidence."

"Hi, Susan."

"Hi, Lexy. How are you? You still trying to get that penuche recipe out of me?"

Lexy laughed. She loved Susan's penuche fudge and had been trying to coerce the recipe out of her for years, but the other woman wouldn't give it up. Said it was an old family secret. "Yes, but that's not why I called."

"Okay, what's up?"

You probably heard about the break-in at Wolf's photography the other day."

"Yes, of course. That's very disturbing. I'm having extra locks installed on the fudge shop."

"I was wondering if you saw anything suspicious that morning."

"The police asked me that. I didn't see anything out of the ordinary. I certainly didn't notice anyone breaking in. But they probably came in through the back where no one could see, and I don't go out back too often."

Lexy's heart sank. "Oh. Okay."

"Why do you ask?"

"I catered the desserts at Regis Banks' birthday party and the pictures from that were stolen from Wolf's, so I kind of have a vested interest. I was hoping you might have seen something."

"Sorry. I didn't see a thing. The only thing out of the ordinary that day was the little ball of fluff that came to the shop door."

"Ball of fluff?"

"Yes. I found a tiny orange dog yipping at the shop door. I heard the noise, opened the door and barely noticed it, the thing was so small. And all fur. Anyway, I was about to scoop it up when some lady came running down the street in stilettos, yelling about falafels. I tried to tell her we didn't sell those, just fudge and candy. Then she grabbed the dog and ran off."

Lexy's heart turned over in her chest. "Falafels? Wait a minute, are you sure she wasn't calling the dog Farfel?"

160

"Oh, maybe that's what it was!" Susan's laugh rang through the line. "That's me—always thinking about food. I got a customer here. Was there anything else?

"No, you've been very helpful. Thanks for calling."

"Okay, don't forget to stop by. I'm having a sale next week!"

Lexy hung up and noticed all eyes were on her.

"Well?" Nans stood by the whiteboard, her hands on her hips.

"Susan didn't see Larry or Evelyn there that morning, but she did see someone else," Lexy said.

"Who?" Ruth, Ida, Helen and Norman chorused.

"Olivia Banks."

***

"Well, that's just dandy," Nans said. "Now we have too many killers!

"Are you sure it was Olivia who Susan saw?" Ruth frowned at Lexy. "Does she know her enough to recognize her?"

Lexy pressed her lips together. "Well, she didn't actually *say* it was Olivia, but the dog she described, and the name the woman called it sounds like Olivia's Pomeranian. Olivia doted on that dog, so I'm sure she wouldn't let someone else take it downtown."

Helen sighed. "We're going to have to come up with a way to weed the suspects out one by one."

"Sure," Ida slurped some coffee. "But how?"

Nans tapped her index finger against pursed lips. "We'll have to go back to basics—means, motive and opportunity."

"We knew they all had motive," Norman said.

"And means?" Helen asked. "Once we find out what Winston was poisoned with it might help us rule out one of the three, but until then we'll have to look at opportunity."

"They all had opportunity to switch the ice creams on Regis, but what about Winston?" Ruth added. "Evelyn would be the big favorite there since she'd have the most opportunity, being his wife and all."

"I guess we need to find out where all three of them were the morning Winston died," Nans said.

"How do you propose we do that?" Lexy asked.

"Good old detective work … and lots of baked goods."

Lexy made a face. "Lots of baked goods? I'm going to go broke at the rate we're giving away desserts."

"Now, Lexy," Nans clucked. "You know that no one gets suspicious about us coming around and asking questions when we bring pastries. It's one of our best tactics."

Lexy sighed. It was true, people seemed to be happy to spill their guts if you plied them with cookies and brownies.

"Here's what we're going to do." Nans raised her marker over the empty section at the end of the whiteboard. "We'll make another trip to the Farmer's Market … but not to see Larry. We'll have to talk to someone else, an impartial witness that can verify if Larry and Evelyn were there yesterday morning. Does anyone here know someone who works there?"

Norman raises his hand. "I do."

"Great, do you know them well enough to talk to about Larry and Evelyn?" Nans asked. "You can put your hand down, dear."

Norman looked at his hand and then lowered it. "Yes, Judy works at the paper part-time. I'm sure she'd tell us. I don't even think we'd have to bribe her with cookies."

163

"Perfect," Nans scribbled on the whiteboard. "Now what about Olivia? Who can we ask about her?"

"I could ask around the *Fur Fun K9 Center*," Lexy offered. "I don't really know anyone there though, and it might be a bit awkward."

"Maybe we should go in and do our old lady act," Ida suggested.

"Old lady act?" Norman raised his brows.

Nans shrugged. "Sometimes when we want to get information, we just act like doddering old ladies. You'd be surprised at how many people spill their guts to old ladies without thinking anything of it."

"Wow," Norman looked at her in awe. "You really have this thing down pat. I could use you guys to help me with the research on some of my newspaper articles."

Nans tilted her head. "You know, maybe we could help each other out with research on future cases. We could do some field work and you could use your resources down at the paper."

Normans face lit up. "I'd like that! Maybe I'd even get to do something heroic for once—I always wanted to save someone or help someone, but it hasn't happened yet."

Norman's expression dimmed and Lexy's heart tugged just a little for him.

"That's great for *future* cases," Ruth's voice dripped with sarcasm. "But can we get on with discussing *this* case?"

"Right," Nans turned to the whiteboard and wrote 'old lady act at *K9 Center*'. "I think we should start with these two tasks and see if that eliminates any of the suspects, then figure out where to go from there."

Chapter Sixteen

They split up into two teams. Lexy, Norman and Ida were tasked with talking to Judy at the Farmer's Market and Nans, Ruth and Helen went to ask about Olivia at the *Fur Fun K9 Center*.

Lexy's team took Norman's car. Lexy sat in the back so Norman could grill Ida about her investigative techniques on the way. Lexy ignored the conversation as she chewed on her thumbnail and wondered if her bakery would suffer because of all the time she was spending away from running it. She made a mental note to give Cassie and their part-time girl, Haley, a bonus for extra work they had to do in her absence.

They pulled up in front of the Farmer's Market and piled out of the car.

"Now remember," Ida leaned toward Norman, her voice barely above a whisper, "don't make it too obvious how eager we are to find out where Evelyn was that morning. We don't want to let on that we are *investigating*."

Norman's eyes went wide and he nodded like a puppy eager to please its master.

They went inside and Norman looked around for Judy while Ida and Lexy pretended to be interested in the watermelons.

"There she is, over by the onions." Norman nodded toward a petite brunette arranging signs on a display that was loaded with onions, garlic and potatoes.

"Let's go over slowly," Ida advised and Norman started to walk at a snail's pace.

"Not that slow." Ida rolled her eyes at Lexy.

Norman increased to a normal pace. Judy looked up as they approached, recognized Norman and smiled.

"Hi, Norman. What brings you here?"

"Oh, we were just shopping for some ..." Norman hesitated and shot Ida a look of panic.

"Sweet potatoes," Ida said, picking up one of the orange spuds in the bin in front of her and inspecting it. "Gonna make a sweet potato pie."

"That sound delicious," Judy said. "Is this your grandma?"

"Ummm ... no ..." Norman stuttered.

"I'm a friend of Norman's grandma and this here is Lexy." Ida nodded toward Lexy.

"I'm Judy," the girl said pointing to her name tag.

"We know some of the managers here ... Larry and Evelyn," Ida said before Judy could get away.

"Oh, they're real nice," Judy said, favoring them with a perky dimpled smile.

"I didn't see them here yesterday morning." Ida eyed Judy out of the corner of her eye.

"I know Evelyn wasn't here because she was already gone to the Organic Growers Convention in Houston." Judy chewed her bottom lip for a few seconds. "Nope, Larry wasn't here either. I remember because we had a problem with the spaghetti squash and he was the only one that could fix it, but no one could find him."

"Oh," Ida feigned interest in a plump Vidalia onion. "When did Evelyn leave for the convention?"

"Oh, she left two days ago. I remember because she was leaving on my day off ... of course she had to cut her trip short and fly back when Winston ... you know." Judy looked down at the floor.

"Hello, ladies." Larry had come up behind Lexy and was regarding them with narrowed eyes. "Nice to see you again."

"Hi, Larry," Ida smiled and held up a sweet potato. "Just coming to get some of these wonderful potatoes for a pie."

"I thought I heard you asking about Evelyn," he said sharply.

Judy's eyes darted from Larry to Ida to Lexy. "I was just telling—"

Ida cut her off. "We were telling Judy how much we enjoyed talking to you and Evelyn the other day."

"And we wanted to tell you how sorry we were about Winston," Lexy added.

A shadow passed across Larry's face. Sorrow? Guilt? Lexy couldn't tell which.

"Thanks." His face turned hard. "We didn't see eye to eye on a lot of things, but he was still my brother."

"Of course. You must be terribly upset," Ida soothed.

Larry nodded then looked pointedly at Judy. "The grapefruit display needs straightening."

"Yes, of course." Judy nodded at Norman, Lexy and Ida before scurrying off.

"I can help you take these potatoes up." Larry put the potatoes Ida had been fondling into a bag. "Do you need anything else for your pie?"

"No, that should do it."

Larry escorted them to the cashier, Ida paid for the potatoes and they piled back into Norman's car.

Ida half-turned in the seat so she could see both Lexy and Norman. "Was it just me, or did you guys get the impression Larry was trying to get rid of us?"

"He was definitely trying to get rid of us ... and he didn't seem too happy we were talking about him and Evelyn to Judy."

Norman's brows shot up to his hairline. "Almost as if he had something to hide."

Ida nodded. "At least we discovered one thing. Evelyn most likely didn't do it because she'd been gone for a whole day before Winston died."

"But Larry could have," Norman added. "According to Judy, he wasn't at the Farmer's Market that morning."

Lexy's heart sank. Could Larry be the killer? She liked Larry and didn't want it to be him. "That doesn't prove he killed Winston."

"Of course not," Ida said. "But it brings up the question of where he was that morning."

Lexy nodded. "We need to dig deeper and find out if he has an alibi ... or if he was with his brother."

"And there's another question, too," Ida said.
"What's that?" Norman asked.

Ida held up the bag she'd brought from the store. "What the heck am I going to do with these potatoes?"

***

"It sure is pretty out here. No wonder so many people are opposed to the retail development." Nans stood beside Ruth's Olds, stretching her back as she gazed out over the lush fields of grass and wild flowers.

"Copy that," Ruth said, then reached into the car and grabbed the bag of Snickerdoodles they'd scoffed from Lexy's bakery.

"I remember when this was a working farm," Helen added as they walked toward the door. "There used to be cows, goats and horses. Momma got all her vegetables from the farm stand."

"Oh, that's too bad it's gone to ruin." Nans held the door open for Helen.

The three of them looked around the lobby of the *K9 Center*.

"Where should we start?" Ruth asked.

"Let's find someone who works here ... and who looks like they want to talk."

They turned the corner and walked up to the desk to the doggie daycare. Behind it, a blonde with short curly hair sat staring at the computer.

"Hello," Nans said brightly.

"Can I help you?"

"I'm Mona and this is Ruth and Helen." Nans opened the cookie bag and angled it toward the blonde. "Cookie?"

The girl glanced into the bag uncertainly, then up at Nans before dipping her hand in and pulling out a cookie. "Do you have a question about the doggie daycare?"

"Were doing an article on the *K9 Center* for the Tribune," Helen coughed. "We're just looking around to get some background info."

"Ruth here does the society pages," Nans nodded at Ruth.

"Oh." The girl gave them a disinterested look as she munched her cookie.

"Yes, and I hear you have a member of high society that comes here," Ruth said.

"We do?"

"Yes, Olivia Banks."

"Oh, yeah." The girl waved her hand. "She's here all the time. Has a couple of Pomeranians that do agility. Really cute and fast, too. The dogs, I mean ... not Olivia."

"Right. We were wondering if she had a regular schedule. We might want to come when we can snap a picture," Ruth said.

The girl scrunched her face up. "She really doesn't have a set schedule, but if you want to get a photo of her today, you've come way too early. She never gets in before noon."

Nans raised her brows at the others. "Oh, thanks. I guess we'll just mosey around and get a feel for the place for our article," Nans turned and winked at Helen and Ruth.

"Thanks," Helen said to the girl.

"You're welcome. Have a nice day," the girl called after them as they walked off.

"Well, how do you like them apples?" Nans reached into the bag of cookies, then held it out for Ruth and Helen, who both took a cookie.

"That doesn't help us at all," Helen crunched into her cookie.

"Nope, we'll have to find out what Olivia does each morning if we want to rule her out by establishing an alibi." Nans held the door open and they spilled out into the sunshine.

"Let's find out if the other team had better success." Nans rummaged in her oversized purse, then pulled out her cell phone, stabbed at the screen and put it up to her ear.

"Hello, Ida?"

"Hi, Mona ... how did you guys make out?" Ida's voice crackled in Nans ear.

"It was a bust for us. What about you?"

"We got some interesting information." The excitement in Ida's voice carried over the line,

174

making Nans tingle with anticipation. "We're on our way back to your place now to compare notes."

"We'll meet you there." Nans broke into a sprint, gesturing for Ruth and Helen to hurry it up as she yelled into the phone. "Last ones there have to clean up after coffee!"

***

"If what Judy told you is true, we can rule out Evelyn." Nans marched over to the whiteboard and drew a line through Evelyn's name.

"We may want to double check with the Organic Growers Convention and make sure she was really there." Helen dipped her Snickerdoodle in her cup of coffee. Lexy noticed she didn't bother to clean up the few drops that sloshed over onto the table.

Nans nodded. "Good idea, it pays to be thorough."

"I'll call them," Ruth said and Nans made a note on the whiteboard.

"Evelyn still could have done it," Helen said. "She could have put something in leftovers that she knew Winston would eat later on. That would be perfect, actually, because if he ate it while she was away, that would give her an alibi."

"No, I don't think she would have done that," Ruth crunched into a cookie, ignoring the crumbs that fell on the table in front of her. "It's too risky—what if someone came over to visit and ate the food?"

Nans nodded, then chugged down her coffee. She brought the cup to the kitchen counter, opened the cabinet and pulled out a clean one which she filled with more coffee.

Lexy's mouth pursed into a thin line. "You can use the same cup, you know, Nans."

"Oh, I know, but, since you guys have to clean up ..."

Lexy sighed. They'd pulled up in front of the Retirement Center at the same time as Nans, Ruth and Helen, but the old ladies had proven to be faster at getting out of the car and sprinting through the halls.

"So, now we need to figure out where Larry and Olivia were that morning," Norman said.

"Larry was acting awfully funny at the Farmer's Market," Lexy said.

"Yeah, almost as if he didn't want us asking questions," Ida added.

"And Judy did say he was supposed to be there, but didn't show up," Norman pointed out.

"Which means he deviated from his routine," Nans said. "Too bad he lives in that cabin in the woods. We can't ask a doorman or servant where he was."

"Where's his cabin?" Norman asked.

"Out on Mountain Road," Ruth tapped on her iPad that she'd placed on the table in front of her. "I looked it up earlier. Nice place, but simple.

She slid the iPad across the table to Norman.

"Remote with no neighbors, so we can't ask them, either," Helen said.

"Maybe we should focus on Winston's place," Ruth offered. "See if one of them paid him a visit."

Helens phone chirped. She pulled it out of her purse, looked at it and then rolled her eyes. "It's Stan. He's been texting me and posting on my Facebook timeline. I knew we shouldn't have gone over there the other day."

"Now, Helen," Nans soothed. "That was for the good of the case. We all have to make sacrifices."

"What's so bad about Stan? He's not bad looking, he's rich and he sure does seem to be smitten with you," Lexy said.

Helen made a face. "Jeez, Lexy. At my age the last thing I need is a man hanging around and spoiling all my fun. I'll just text him back that I'm not available."

"Wait a second!" Nans yelled.

Helen poised her finger over the phone, her left brow lifted at Nans.

"Maybe we should invite him over. He was friends with Winston ... he might know something about his death," Nans said.

"Honestly, Mona, I really don't want to encourage him."

"Please?" Nans gave Helen her most endearing look. "It might be our only chance."

"You can lure him over with some of Lexy's Snickerdoodles. One more place setting won't be too much, especially since we don't have to clean it up." Ruth smirked at Ida.

Helen let out an exaggerated sigh. "Okay. Fine."

She typed into her phone. A few seconds later her phone dinged. Her shoulders slumped as she read the text. "He'll be right over.

Stan must not have been very far away, because no sooner had Nans, Ruth and Helen moved the whiteboard back to Nans spare room to hide it, when a knock sounded at the door. Nans ushered him in and made a fuss over giving him coffee and pastries.

Lexy noticed the sly smile on Nans' lips as she made sure extra crumbs fell on the table when she transferred a scone to Stan's plate. Nans got an extra chair from the living room and everyone sat down.

"Helen, I was hoping you'd like to go to lunch today." Stan gazed at Helen as if no one else was in the room.

"Oh, I don't know ..." Helen started out, then jumped as if someone had kicked her under the table. *Probably Nans*, Lexy thought.

"That would be lovely," she said, fixing Nans with a nasty glare.

"Say, Stan, did you hear about Winston Banks?" Nans didn't waste any time getting to the point.

Stan looked down at his scone. "Yes, I was sorry to hear about him. Isn't it funny that we'd just been talking about him a couple of days before? I guess the stress of his extracurricular activities got to him."

"Yeah, funny," Ruth said. "Life is full of little coincidences."

"It sure is," Stan replied. "In fact, I had just seen him that morning at the club."

Lexy's ears perked up. "Oh, really? Did he seem sick?"

"No, not at all. That's why I was surprised when I heard the news." Stan sipped his coffee. "I mean, it couldn't have been more than an hour or two later that he died."

"But that was in the morning," Nans said. "I didn't realize people went to the club so early."

"Oh, normally no one goes that early. But on Wednesdays they have the best eggs benedict. That's why I was there and why Winston was there, too."

Nans raised a brow at him. "So, you ate breakfast together?"

Stan shook his head. "Not together. We were at different tables, and now I regret that I didn't go over and talk to him, but he was having what looked like a heated conversation and I didn't want to interrupt."

"A heated conversation?" Nans leaned across the table, her eyes focused on Stan's face. "Who with?"

"With his brother. Larry Banks."

Chapter Seventeen

Lexy managed to make her get-away after Stan dropped the bomb about Winston eating breakfast with Larry. She had work to do at the bakery, not the least of which was resupplying the pastry case since Nans had been using it for her own personal inventory of bribe material.

As she worked, baking and waiting on customers, she considered the news about Larry breakfasting with Winston.

Did Larry kill Winston? He certainly had enough reasons, but she still couldn't picture him as a killer. Lexy wondered what they'd been fighting about. Had it been important enough for Larry to poison Winston's breakfast?

Lexy was just putting some freshly baked lemon squares in the pastry case when Nans, Ruth, Ida and Helen marched through the door, dressed to the nines.

"What's the occasion?" Lexy eyed the colorful polyester pantsuits the ladies wore.

"We're going to the club for dinner," Nans said.

"Winston's club?" Lexy asked.

"Yep, Stan arranged for us to get in and even called his chef friend especially for us," Ruth slid her eyes toward Helen. "Of course, Helen had to take one for the home team."

Lexy raised a brow at Helen.

"I agreed to go on a date with Stan next Saturday."

"Sorry, Helen," Lexy said.

"Not as sorry as you're gonna be," Ida wagged her finger at Lexy. "You and Norman skedaddled out of there and left me to do all the cleanup."

Lexy grimaced, "I know. Sorry. I'll make it up to you, I promise. I just made lemon squares—do you want one?"

Ida shook her head. "You can't bribe me with pastries. Besides, I don't want to spoil my dinner."

"We have reservations at seven, so we swung by to see if you want to go with us," Ruth said.

Lexy glanced down at her flour-covered jeans and tee-shirt, then looked at the clock. It was almost six o'clock. Jack was working late and she had planned a quick supper of cereal. A gourmet meal sounded much better and she'd have just enough time to go home and change.

"Sounds good. Just let me lock up and we can go to my place and then head over."

The club was as posh as Lexy had expected it to be, with mahogany paneled walls, white linen tablecloths, crystal glasses and gold rimmed cream colored china. Lexy turned over her fork and, sure enough, it was stamped sterling silver on the back. The light from the ornate crystal chandelier overhead glinted off the tines as she put it back on the table.

The black acoustic tile ceiling and sumptuous burgundy colored rug did a great job of absorbing the sound. Lexy could only hear the muted tones of hushed conversations and the faint tinkling of silverware on china plates.

After they'd gotten their drinks and ordered both the appetizer and their meals, Nans proposed a toast.

"To catching killers." Her green eyes sparkled as they all clinked wine glasses. Lexy noticed a man at the next table give them a funny look. Maybe Nans shouldn't have said 'killers' quite so loudly.

The waitress came with a plate loaded with snail shells. Escargot. Ida daintily took one with a thin, long-tined fork and passed the plate to Lexy. Lexy declined, passing the plate over to Ruth.

"You don't want one?" Ruth asked.

"No."

"They're good." Nans took the plate from Ruth. "These are loaded with butter and garlic."

"I'll save the room for my prime rib."

"Excuse me." The man who had looked over when Nans made the toast leaned toward them in his chair. "Aren't you gals *The Ladies Detective Club*?"

Nans puffed up with pride. "Why, yes we are. How did you know?"

"You solved a case for my cousin about a year ago. Did a right fine job, too." He pushed his chair closer and lowered his voice. "The police couldn't figure it out, but you ladies nailed it."

"Why, thank you." Nans patted her lip with the white cloth napkin.

Ida, Ruth and Helen beamed at the man as they chewed on their snails.

"Are you on a case now?" he asked.

"Why, as a matter of fact we are," Nans said in a hushed voice. "We're looking into the murders of Regis and Winston Banks."

"Murders?" His hazel eyes widened. "But I thought Regis died from a food allergy and Winston died of a heart attack."

"That's what the killer wants you to think," Ida said.

"Oh, how fascinating," the man said. "I saw Winston just that morning right here at the club."

Nans twisted in her chair to face him. "You did?"

The man nodded. "He was here with his brother. An odd fellow, that Larry Banks. He hardly ever comes here because he only likes to eat organic food, but the eggs here are local from pastured chickens, so he's joined Winston a few times for breakfast on Wednesday's. He brings his own organic juices, though ... sometimes tries to push them off on the rest of us."

Nans' radar perked up. "And did he bring his own juice on Wednesday?"

"Yep. A big bottle of something thick and green. He asked the waiter for a champagne glass and poured it right in for Winston."

Nans narrows her eyes at the man. "Did you notice if Winston drank it?"

The man tilted his head, rubbing his chin. "I'm not sure ... no, wait. He did drink it."

"Are you sure?" Ida asked.

The man scooted his chair even closer, lowering his voice even further. "I don't know if you noticed that Winston had some sort of phobia about having his hands dirty ... he used those wet naps all the time."

"We did notice that," Nans said.

The man grimaced. "Well, I know it's kind of childish, but a few of us had a running bet as to how many wet naps he would use. He used five that day and I won the bet. That's how I know he drank the drink because when I looked at the table for the final count, I remember the champagne

185

glass at his seating was empty—only a film of green sludge remained on the sides."

***

Lexy pulled into her driveway behind Jack's truck and hopped out of the car. She was excited to see him. Of course, she was excited any time she got to see Jack, but tonight she also couldn't wait to tell him about the latest development in the Banks' case.

Lexy opened the door, expecting the usual, overzealous greeting from Sprinkles. Her heart sank when the dog didn't come.

What the heck?

"We're in here," Jack yelled from the kitchen.

Lexy crossed the living room to the kitchen where Jack was waiting with a glass of red wine. Sprinkles was busy gobbling up the last of a piece of steak from her dog bowl.

"So that's why Sprinkles didn't greet me," Lexy said, accepting the wine and a quick kiss.

Sprinkles swallowed the last bite, looked up in surprise at Lexy, and then launched herself at Lexy's knees, almost causing her to spill the wine. Lexy put the glass down and bent to pet the dog.

"Yes, I'm glad to see you," she said to Sprinkles, then looked back up at Jack, "and you, too."

"Same here," Jack grinned at her over his wine glass and Lexy's heart did a somersault. That boyish grin always got to her. "How was your fancy dinner?"

Lexy stood up. "Very enlightening."

"Oh, really?" Jack's left brow ticked up a fraction of an inch.

"I think we might have discovered who killed Regis and Winston." Lexy told him how Larry had had a fight with Winston at breakfast that morning and supplied him with a special juice.

"And I suppose Nans and the ladies have worked out a motive," Jack said.

"Yes, actually. Larry had several. First off, he was opposed to the way *Banks Development* did business, so getting Regis and then Winston out of the way would give him and Olivia controlling interests."

"Don't tell me you think he'll kill Olivia next to get everything."

Lexy pressed her lips together. She hadn't considered that. Would he?

"I was kidding," Jack said. "So what are his other motives?"

"Well, the second one would be to get more of the Banks money, of course."

"How would he get more of the Banks money?" Jack's brow creased. "I doubt Winston willed his inheritance to Larry."

"That brings me to the third and probably most compelling reason." Lexy paused for effect. "Larry and Winston's wife, Evelyn, were having an affair."

Jack's eyebrows shot up to his hairline. "An affair? How do you know that?"

"We did some surveillance and we have pictures."

"Maybe it was Evelyn."

"She has an alibi for that morning—she was away at a convention."

"Hmm... that's certainly interesting. I'll have to get those from Nans. You guys might be on to something."

Pride swelled in Lexy's chest. "So you admit I'm getting pretty good at this investigating stuff."

Jack draped his arm around her shoulders and nuzzled her ear. "Among other things."

Lexy giggled. "We could go upstairs and you could test me on those other things."

Jack removed his arm. "Actually, I was referring to cleaning out my house. I want to get that finished up soon so we can put it on the market this summer. That's the best time to sell a house."

Lexy's shoulders slumped. "I guess I have been neglecting that. I promise to help tomorrow night. I have agility class at five, but after that I'm all yours."

"Great. It's a date, then." Jack swilled down his wine. "If you see Nans tomorrow, tell her I want those pictures … oh, and the toxicology test she ordered should be back from the lab tomorrow. That might give us some ideas on how to prove Larry is the killer … if he actually is."

"I'm sure she'll be happy about that."

"Yeah, and don't let her forget, Mike is expecting an apple pie for that."

Lexy laughed. "I just hope she doesn't expect me to bake it. She has more of a talent for those than I do."

Jack took the wine glass out of her hand and set it on the counter, then pulled her toward the living room. The glint in his eye kicked her heartbeat up a notch.

"I know that you have some talents that are much more interesting than baking apple pies … and now would be a perfect time for you to show them to me."

Chapter Eighteen

"Things have actually been going pretty smoothly without you here," Cassie said as she creamed together shortening, sugar and eggs.

Lexy frowned at the flour, baking soda, cream of tartar and salt mixture she was sifting together. She didn't like the way that sounded—almost as if she wasn't needed in her own bakery.

"I mean, it's still better when you *are* here," Cassie added after noticing the look on Lexy's face. "And we can use the extra help to replenish our supply of Snickerdoodles."

Lexy laughed as she handed the bowl of dry ingredients to Cassie.

"I know that Nans thinks giving people cookies will get them to open up and talk." She poured some sugar and cinnamon into a shallow bowl, mixing the two together with a fork. "But the truth is, I think the ladies have been eating most of them."

Cassie laughed. "No doubt."

The girls dug teaspoon shaped balls out of the batter, rolled the balls in the cinnamon and sugar mixture and set them on a cookie sheet. Lexy could almost taste the buttery cinnamon flavor of the cookies as she slid the sheet into the oven.

The bells over the front door to the shop chimed.

"Your turn," Cassie said not taking her eyes off the red velvet cake she was frosting.

"Got it." Lexy wiped the flour off her cherry pattern vintage 1950s apron and headed for the front room. She should have known who it would be—Nans, Ruth, Ida and Helen. It was almost as if they had a sixth sense and knew she'd just put in a fresh batch of Snickerdoodles.

"You guys are a little early." Lexy made a big show of looking at her watch. "The Snickerdoodles won't be out for six more minutes."

Nans chuckled and helped herself to a coffee from the self-serve station. "Oh, we didn't come for cookies. We were just discussing the new developments in the case and wanted to make sure everyone was on the same page."

"We knew you'd be working today, so we thought we'd come to you," Ruth added.

"Although, fortifying ourselves with some pastries wouldn't hurt," Ida eyed the pastry case.

Lexy couldn't help but smile. "Okay. You guys get coffee and I'll fix up a plate."

She opened the pastry case and pulled out some of yesterday's scones and brownies. If the ladies were going to eat all her profits, she might as well give them the day old items she was going to have to pack up for the soup kitchen anyway.

The four ladies settled at a table, the white ceramic coffee mugs that Lexy supplied for customers who ate in the cafe sitting in front of them. Lexy put the tray on the table and they each selected a pastry, putting their napkins primly on their laps and taking a nibble.

"Okay. Let's get to it." Nans brushed crumbs from her hand onto her plate.

"I checked out Evelyn's alibi and verified she was a thousand miles away at the Organic Growers conference, so she couldn't have put anything in Winston's food that morning or even the day before," Ruth said.

"But she and Larry could have been in on it together and the conference gives her the perfect alibi. Maybe that's why she went." Ida broke off a piece of scone and popped it into her mouth.

"Either way, I'm willing to bet Larry put something in that drink. But, of course, the glass has been washed by now, so we can't test it," Nans said. "Anyone have any ideas on what we can do to get some evidence against him?"

"We've already proven he had motive and opportunity." Helen ticked the two items off on her fingers. "I guess we just need to prove the means."

"Which we can do by catching him with the poison," Ida added.

"Except we don't know what the poison was," Ruth pointed out.

"Jack said the toxicology report should be in today ... oh, and you owe Mike an apple pie," Lexy said.

Nans grimaced. "I guess I do. Did you tell Jack about Larry giving Winston special juice at breakfast?"

"I did," Lexy said. "And I also told him about Larry and Evelyn's affair. He wants copies of those pictures. He seemed very interested in our theories."

Nans beamed with pride. "Ruth, can you email Jack the pictures? I'll just give him a call and let him know we are sending them *and* see if the toxicology report came back yet."

Nans reached into the gigantic beige patent leather purse that hung on the back of her chair, pulled out her iPhone and called Jack.

"Hi, Jack, it's Mona. I was wondering about that toxicology report ..."

Everyone at the table watched Nans expectantly.

194

"Yes, I know I have to bake a pie," Nans rolled her eyes and made circling motions with her hand.

"Okay, that's the only thing that came up?" Nans pulled out a pen and started to write something, then paused her pen in mid-air.

"What do you mean our theory just got shot?" Her forehead creased into dozens of wrinkles.

Lexy watched as three pairs of gray eyebrows rose.

"Tried to kill him? But how do you know that wasn't an accident?"

Ruth, Ida and Helen's eyes got a little bigger and they put their pastries down on their plates.

"Jiminy Cricket, that sure does change things. I'll get my people on it right away." Nans disconnected, a look of worry on her face.

"Well, what is it?" Ruth demanded.

"It looks like Larry might not be the killer after all."

"What? Why do you say that?" Helen asked.

"Jack just told me that Larry was found in his cabin unconscious. He was rushed to the hospital with carbon monoxide poisoning."

"How does that prove he's not the killer?" Lexy asked.

"When the police heard about another Banks family member in critical condition, they got suspicious and went to his cabin to investigate. He has a kerosene heater that's vented to the outside—someone had plugged up the flu with rags!"

"So someone tried to kill him on purpose and probably thought it would look like another accident," Helen said. "I bet they were going to go back and take the rags out later on, so everyone would have thought there was a leak from the heater. Goodness knows there have been enough reports of carbon monoxide leaks in the papers so no one would think anything of it."

"This sure does put things in a different perspective." Nans drummed her fingers on the table.

"It looks like someone is killing off the Banks family and that leaves only one member that hasn't been targeted," Ruth said.

"Olivia!" Lexy, Ida and Helen said in unison.

Nans nodded. "That's right. But the question is … is she the next victim, or the killer?"

***

"My vote is that she's the killer," Ida bit into her brownie, then scowled at Lexy. "Are these fresh?"

"They're less than twenty-four hours old." It was true, by Lexy's calculation they were twenty-three hours and fifty-four minutes old.

"She *was* one of our primary suspects before we found out about the breakfast meeting with Larry and Winston," Helen pointed out.

"But that drink seemed like the perfect way to poison Winston," Lexy said. "When would Olivia have had a chance to poison him?"

"Maybe Olivia and Larry were in on it together and then after they killed Winston, she tried to do away with Larry." Ida raised her brows over her coffee cup.

"Hmm ... maybe." Ruth slurped her coffee noisily.

"Did you find out what the poison was?" Helen turned to Nans. "If we know then that could help us narrow down who had the means to use it."

Nans looked down at the piece of paper. "Aconite. Have any of you heard of it?"

Ida nodded. "I have. It comes from a plant called wolfsbane. Very toxic."

"A plant? Does it grow around here?" Nans asked.

Lexy's heart kicked. "Wait a minute. Do you mean like an herb?"

"Yes, exactly. It *is* an herb," Ida said. "It has lots of medicinal uses, but you have to be very careful with it as it can be deadly. I suppose it *could* grow around here, but I haven't heard of it too much in the wild. If you wanted to grow it yourself, though …"

"I saw Olivia with a book on herbs when I was at the *Fur Fun K9 Center*." The words rushed out of Lexy's mouth.

Ruth sucked in a breath. "So she would have had the knowledge about how to use it as a poison as well as how to grow it."

"And those stems I saw in the dumpster …" Lexy stared at the others as she let the words trail off.

"And don't forget your friend saw her the morning the photographer's shop was broken into." Helen reminded Lexy.

"That's right. *And* she sat next to Regis at the party, so she was probably afraid there was a picture of her switching the ice creams!"

"I could see why she'd kill Regis and maybe even Winston, but why Larry?" Nans asked. "If the reason for the killings was that she didn't want the Meadow Lane land developed, she could have spared him. He wouldn't have developed the land."

"According to the terms of the will, shares of stock owned by each of the brothers would have reverted to Olivia upon their death. So, with her father and brothers out of the way she'd have controlling interest in *Banks Development*. Maybe she has grander plans than just stopping the Meadow Lane Development," Ruth said.

"Or maybe she didn't want Larry getting in the way of her and Steve's smuggling business," Ida offered.

"But with the million she inherited, does she really need to smuggle drugs?" Lexy asked.

Nans gave Lexy a look and the three other ladies twittered. "Lexy, I think you've led too sheltered of a life. Drug smuggling can be a lot more lucrative than one-million-dollars."

"Maybe, but she can't be that smart if all her efforts to make the murders look like accidents keep getting exposed." Lexy picked a chocolate chip cookie—now a full day old—from the plate and crunched into it.

"True, and by now she'll know her unsuccessful attempt to kill Larry has been exposed." Helen eyed them all warily. "Which could make her very dangerous."

"That's right." Nans nodded. "She's probably getting desperate to cover her tracks, so we'd better proceed with caution."

Helen nodded. "There's no telling to what extreme she'll go to keep from being discovered."

Nans leaned across the table, her face grim. "If we're right, she's already killed twice, so there's nothing to stop her from killing again."

Chapter Nineteen

Lexy could hardly keep her mind on work the rest of the day. Nans and the ladies had worked out a plan to try and expose Olivia. Ruth and Helen would put their internet skills to use trying to dig up anything they could on the *Fur Fun K9 Center* or the owner, Steve.

Nans and Ida planned to hit the streets, asking their network of informants if they knew anything about a drug smuggling operation out of the *K9 Center*. Lexy's job was to go to her agility class just like usual and try to dig up something on Olivia.

At five o'clock, she closed up the shop and drove home to get Sprinkles, eating the lemon square she'd grabbed out of the case for supper on the way.

A tingle of nerves ate away at her confidence as she drove toward the *K9 Center*. If Olivia was the killer, then maybe it wasn't such a good idea to be digging up information on her.

Then again, what could Olivia possibly do to her in a place full of people and dogs?

"Maybe I should call Jack and let him know, just in case," she said out loud to Sprinkles, who was panting happily in the passenger seat. "What do you think?"

Sprinkles gave her an 'are-you-crazy?' look.

"Right. Bad idea."

Lexy took the turn onto Meadow Road, the lemon square settling in her stomach like a brick.

"I wonder if Nans has an update. She should have called by now." She fished her cell phone out to check. "Oh, that's right. I turned it off so I wouldn't get interrupted while I was baking."

Lexy pressed the button and the phone turned on, then dinged to announce she had a message. It wasn't from Nans. It was from Norman.

She frowned as she hit the button to listen to the message. "I wonder what he wants?"

"Hi, Lexy. I was doing some surveillance on our suspects and Olivia is acting pretty strange. I've followed her to that old farm on Meadow Road. I'm going in to see what she's up to."

Lexy's heart froze—they hadn't yet told Norman about the attempt on Larry's life. He had no idea Olivia was the killer!

She fumbled with the phone to press the call back button, her grip tightening on the steering wheel as she waited for it to connect. Her gut churned when it passed straight to voice mail—he must have his phone turned off so he could stalk Olivia without having it ring and alert her!

She pressed down on the accelerator. The farm was only about a half-mile ahead, but there was no time to waste. She had to warn Norman before Olivia killed him, too!

***

Lexy's heart raced as the farmhouse appeared, a small dot on the horizon. As she got closer, she could see Norman's beige car parked in front of the barn.

Should she go in honking her horn to warn him? No, that might panic Olivia and there was no telling what she'd do. Better to sneak up and surprise her from behind.

She cut the engine, gliding to a stop beside Norman's car. Glancing over at Sprinkles, she hesitated a moment. Should she bring the dog or leave her in the car? Better to bring her and make sure she could protect her rather than risk Olivia coming across the car and harming her.

"Shhh! Sprinkles." Lexy instructed the dog to be quiet and Sprinkles cocked her head to one side as if she understood. Lexy grabbed her leash and led her out the driver's side.

Closing the door quietly behind her, she crept up to the old barn. The sliding barn door was cracked open about a foot. Lexy stood just outside it, straining to hear. The sound of a whip-poorwill broke the silence of the forest, followed by the lonely call of a mourning dove. Squirrels scurried in the dried leaves next to the barn.

A creak sounded from inside.

Was Norman in there?

Lexy realized the old barn would be the perfect place to store drugs ... or even make them. No wonder Olivia and Steve didn't want the area developed into a mall.

Slipping into the dim interior of the barn, she waited a few seconds for her eyes to adjust. Sprinkles stood quietly by her side.

In front of her was an aisle flanked by horse stalls on either side. No sign of Norman or Olivia. To the right was a walled off section which must have contained another room and the small silo that was attached to the barn.

She thought she heard muted voices coming from the other side.

She started toward the sounds. An old board creaked as she put her weight on it and she froze in her tracks, her heartbeat hammering in her chest. No one came or yelled out. She continued on, Sprinkles at her side.

Nearing the door to the walled off section, Lexy reached into her bag and pulled out the can of Mace. Sprinkles stopped short, her nose up in the air, sniffing. She looked up at Lexy apologetically, then lurched around the corner of the wall, through a hall and into the round silo room, pulling Lexy with her.

Lexy's heart stopped as she skidded into the room … and face-to-face with Olivia Banks.

Olivia was sitting awkwardly in a chair, Farfel balanced in her lap. Her wide eyes were filled with fear. Doubt bloomed in Lexy's gut. This wasn't the killer's sneer she expected to see on Olivia's face.

Olivia's eyes slid to look at something behind Lexy's left shoulder. Lexy turned in that direction.

Bam!

Pain exploded on the side of Lexy's head and she went down, the can of Mace flying out of her hand and her palms scraping up splinters in the old, rough wooden flooring.

Her vision became fuzzy, her head spinning. A familiar voice cut through the haze.

"You just couldn't stop snooping, could you?"

Lexy rolled on her side and looked up at the figure. Her vision blurred in and out—she couldn't quite make out who it was.

She blinked, clearing her vision enough to see who it was.

"Cora?"

Chapter Twenty

"That's right." Regis Banks personal assistant glared down the barrel of the gun. "You were expecting someone else?"

"Well, actually, I was." Lexy sat up, eyeing the can of Mace only five feet in front of her.

"Don't get any ideas." Cora kicked the can further away.

Something in the corner caught Lexy's eye. It took her a few minutes to realize it was Norman. He lay slumped on the floor facing away from them, his arms and legs tied together with rope.

"Yes, I found him snooping around, too. Apparently, your head is a bit harder than his—he's been out since I hit him," Cora said. "Now stand up and throw your bag over here."

Lexy got on her hands and knees, then wobbled onto her feet. She tossed the bag over, her stomach sinking when Cora picked up the Mace and stuffed it inside. The Mace had been her only weapon.

Cora gestured with the gun for her to sit in a chair beside Olivia, who Lexy noticed was bound to her own chair with some kind of thick rope. As Lexy backed up, Cora moved over toward the door. Behind her, a small window in the other section of the barn taunted Lexy with a vision of freedom.

In contrast to the dire situation inside the barn, the pastoral scene outside the window was friendly—an old, gnarled oak tree with blue sky and green fields.

Something niggled Lexy's memory.

She knew that scene.

Then it came to her—she'd seen that same tree in the photo in Cora's office!

"That's the picture in your office." Lexy thrust her chin toward the window.

Cora was too smart to turn her back on Lexy. She smiled. "Yes, it is. How observant."

"But how…?" Lexy's brow creased, wondering how Cora had a picture of the view out the barn window of the old farm. Then her mind flashed on Cora's signature on the birthday party catering receipt, her stomach crunching when she remembered Cora's signature had a long last name starting with an 'S'.

'S' as in Silversteen.

Why hadn't she put it all together sooner?

"You're the granddaughter. This is … was … your family farm." Lexy stared at Cora, whose face flushed red with anger.

"That's right. My grandfather was *swindled* out of this land by Regis Banks," Cora spat the words out.

"So, it was *you* who switched the ice creams at the party?"

"Right again. That's why I wanted the timing to be perfect, so he would die before he announced the development of this land … except you were late serving them and almost screwed the whole thing up."

Cora gestured again and Lexy sat in the chair next to Olivia, who had been silently watching the whole exchange. Sprinkles and Farfel snuggled together in a ball on the floor.

Lexy sat down and Sprinkles ran to her, her tail wagging. Cora approached with some rope.

"Put your hands behind you," Cora commanded. Lexy did as told, but as Cora started to bind them Sprinkles began growling, the hair on her neck standing on end.

Cora jumped back, pointing the gun at Sprinkles.

Lexy's stomach twisted. "Don't shoot her!"

"Get her to back off," Cora ground out.

"Sprinkles, sit. It's okay." Sprinkles sat and Lexy almost cried with relief. "Good girl."

"You keep her there and I won't have to shoot her." Cora approached, more cautiously this time.

Sprinkles glanced up at Lexy who shook her head. Thankfully, Sprinkles stayed where she was. Her brown eyes regarded Cora with distrust, but she didn't make a move toward her.

Lexy winced as Cora jerked the ropes tight, cutting into her wrist. All this time, the killer had been Cora!

If only she'd been more observant that day in Cora's office she might have noticed where the picture was from and put two and two together. She remembered the dark smudges on Cora's shoes that day—black, just like the powder that she'd seen spilled in the photography store.

"You stole the photos of the birthday party from Wolf's, too," Lexy said.

"Yes, of course." Cora wrenched the ropes tighter. "I couldn't take a chance that a photo had been taken of me switching those ice creams."

"So that's why they were missing!" Olivia piped up from her chair.

"You were there, too that day, though," Lexy said. "I thought it was you who broke in."

"No. I was supposed to go pick out some pictures of Daddy and my brothers, but I got the appointment date screwed up. I'm not very good at remembering appointments." Olivia's voice cracked. "Our family hasn't been close in recent years and I just wanted pictures of them. I used to

210

be close to my brothers and father when Mom was alive and I miss that. Anyway, I figured there wouldn't be many more pictures of Daddy, but never realized those would actually be the very last ones. And I didn't even get one because when I went back the next day they were missing."

Cora snickered as she got to work on tying Lexy's ankles to the legs of the chair. "Oh poor you, I never got those last pictures of my grandfather, either. He shot himself after your father stole the farm from him."

"So you killed Regis as revenge for his tactics in purchasing the farm land … but did you kill Winston, too?" Lexy figured it couldn't hurt to keep Cora talking while she tried to come up with an escape plan.

Cora smirked. "Of course."

"You *killed* him?" Olivia's forehead creased. "But I thought he died of a heart attack."

"That's what I wanted you to think," Cora boasted. "I used a highly toxic herb that leaves very few traces and has the same symptoms of a heart attack."

"Aconite from the wolfsbane plant," Lexy said.

"How did you know Winston was murdered?" Cora wrinkled her brow at Lexy as she stood up from her rope tying task.

"We just thought it seemed suspicious, two deaths in the family like that. And seeing as Regis' death wasn't natural ..." Lexy shrugged.

"Yes, you and your meddling grandmother," Cora wrinkled her nose. "My only regret is that she and her troupe of old biddies aren't here so I could do away with all of you. If it wasn't for your meddling, no one would have suspected anything!"

Lexy's stomach tightened and she said a silent prayer of thanks that Nans hadn't been with her.

"But how did you know about the aconite? I thought it wouldn't show up on a toxicology screening?" Cora narrowed her eyes at Lexy.

"It won't show up on the regular screening, but we had our suspicions and convinced the police to do an extended screening. The aconite showed up on that." Lexy tilted her head. "It was pretty risky to put aconite in Winston's food before the meeting, though. Anyone could have eaten some and suffered the same fate. Weren't you worried that more than one person would end up dead ... or that Winston might not eat the food you poisoned?"

Cora's laugh sent a chill up Lexy's spine. "You underestimate me. Ingestion isn't the only way to die from aconite. It can also kill you by being absorbed through the skin."

"The skin? But how would you do that?" Lexy's mind flashed to the pile of wet naps in Cora's trash barrel. "Of course! The wet naps!"

"Yes, it took me quite a few tries to perfect my technique." Cora's voice was tinged with pride. "But eventually, I was able to get the aconite oils on a wet nap and seal it back up so no one would notice. Of course, no one really looked at them carefully anyway, and Winston was the only one that ever used them. It would have been the perfect murder if it wasn't for you being so nosy."

"But where did you get the aconite?" Lexy asked.

"Why, I grew it, of course," Cora spread her arms wide. "Right here on this farm. Actually, you helped me, Olivia. I wouldn't have been able to grow it or harvest the oils without your book on herbs."

"So that's why you borrowed it!" Olivia's eyes grew wide. "To poison my own brother."

"At least I made good use of the book," Cora said to Olivia. "Seems like you weren't doing anything with it."

Olivia straightened in her chair. "That's not true!" She looked at them, then snapped her mouth shut.

What's that all about? Was Olivia up to something with herbs, too?

Lexy didn't have time to wonder about what Olivia was up to. There were more pressing matters at hand. Like how to escape from the barn.

"Well, you sure did go to great lengths to get revenge against the Banks family." Lexy said.

Cora's face grew dark. "Yes, I've been planning it for decades. My parents died when I was a baby and Grandpa and Grandma raised me on this farm. The farm had been in my family for several generations and my grandfather sunk into a deep depression once it was stolen from him. He shot himself, and Grandma died shortly after from a broken heart. They were the only family I had … so I decided to take the same type of revenge on the Banks family. Let them see how it is to lose family members, one by one."

"But the police are onto you. They know the deaths were murder now and they'll open an investigation," Lexy said.

"That's right. Your nosiness ruined my plan to make the deaths look accidental." Cora let out an evil laugh, "I even had a backup plan once it came out that someone switched Regis ice cream. That's why I told you Regis had planned to cut Winston out of his will when you came snooping around. To cast suspicion on Winston. Then once he was dead, it would seem like he'd killed Regis and then died from the stress."

Panic lapped at Lexy's stomach as Cora backed toward the door, the gun still trained on them. Lexy's eyes darted around the room, looking for anything she could use as a weapon, but all she saw were old pallets and bales of hay.

Cora zoned the gun in on Olivia. "So now that I've killed Regis, Winston and Larry, you're the last one left."

Olivia gasped. "You killed Larry, too?"

Cora nodded, a self-satisfied smirk on her face.

"Actually, Larry isn't dead," Lexy cut in.

Olivia gasped and looked at Lexy hopefully.

Cora's face crumpled. She swerved the gun toward Lexy. "What do you mean? I stuffed up his flu good and tight."

"I guess you didn't count on someone going over to visit him and getting him out of there before he died. Oh, and the police know someone blocked up the flu." Lexy shrugged. "It's just a matter of time before they trace it to you."

Cora narrowed her eyes at Lexy. "I don't believe you."

"It's true. Why don't you go check before you shoot us? You wouldn't want too many deaths on your hands. That would make for a very long jail sentence."

"Oh, I'm not going to shoot you."

Lexy's brows raised hopefully. Was Cora going to leave them unharmed? Maybe she was only planning on leaving them in here tied up so she could make her getaway?

"Nope, I'm going to burn the barn down with you in it," Cora continued. "My original plan was to just burn Olivia, but since you two came around snooping, I have to burn all of you. Anyway, what's a few more bodies?"

"No, wait. You don't want to do this!" Lexy pleaded.

"I figured you'd say that." Cora backed out the door and stood in the hall, the gun still on them. "Now if you will excuse me, I must get going. I have to push your cars into the pond so no one will think to look for you here before I start the fire. With no cars in the driveway no one is going to care about an old dilapidated dried-out barn burning down. The fire marshal even said it was a fire trap."

"You can't just burn us alive," Lexy's voice quivered.

"Oh, but I think I can."

And with that, she slammed the door shut, locking Lexy, Olivia and Norman in the dark.

Chapter Twenty-One

After a few seconds, Lexy realized that it wasn't totally dark in the silo. A sliver of light cut across the room from a slit of a window about fifteen feet up the side. Lexy blinked back tears as her eyes adjusted to the lack of light.

"Wow, can you believe that?" Norman's excited voice boomed from the corner, causing Lexy to jump. With her eyes now adjusted to the dim lighting, she saw that he was sitting up.

"Are you okay?" Lexy asked.

"Oh, yeah." He worked his wrists back and forth. "I was awake the whole time, but pretended to be asleep so Cora wouldn't see me chewing on the ropes."

He grunted and struggled, then pulled his arms apart, the rope snapping in two. He shrugged his hands free then got to work on his ankles. "I'll get you guys out as soon as I'm free."

"Great. There has to be a way out of here." Lexy wriggled in her chair, craning her neck to study every inch of the room. The only door was the one Cora had just closed and bolted shut.

"I'm sure you already have a good plan," Norman said.

"Plan? Umm … not really." Lexy continued to look around.

"What?" Norman looked up at her. "I thought you and your grandmother had plans to get out of anything."

"Maybe she does, but I don't. Cora took my bag with my cell phone and everything."

"She took ours, too," Olivia cut in. "Car keys, cell phone, even my emery board."

"So this Cora person was the killer the whole time?" Norman asked, still working on the ropes.

"Yes, she was Regis' personal assistant. I guess she must have been planning this for a while." Lexy turned to Olivia. "How long did she work for your father?"

"Two years."

"Two long years of plotting and planning her revenge," Norman said. "That's going to make a great story—"

The sound of a car engine cut him off. Lexy's gut clenched. "That must be her getting rid of one of our cars."

"My fiat is around back," Olivia said. "Cora kidnapped Farfel and told me if I wanted to see her alive to get out here and park around back."

The little orange dog whimpered and snuggled into Olivia's lap.

"That's why I saw you driving like a bat out of hell down Meadow Road." Norman undid the last knot on his ankles. "You were weaving all over the place. I knew something was up."

"So you followed her here," Lexy said. "I got your message and tried to call you, but your phone was off. We thought Olivia was the killer."

"Me?" Olivia sounded hurt.

Another engine started up and Lexy cringed. "Yeah, sorry, but once we realized all the members of your family were being targeted and you were the last one left, we looked at the evidence and it seemed to point to you."

Norman had worked Lexy's wrists free. She rubbed at them, trying to get the circulation back. Sprinkles licked her hand and Lexy petted her head. "Good girl. I'm glad Cora didn't shoot you."

"I can get my legs free. You work on Olivia," Lexy shooed Norman over to Olivia and bent down to work at the knot on her right ankle.

"Wait, what evidence?" Olivia scrunched up her face.

"Well, I had seen you with the herbs book, so we figured you knew about the toxic properties of aconite. Plus, you were seen at the photographer's the morning of the break in and … well … I know there's something secretive going on with you and Steve at the *K9 Center*."

Even though it was now clear Cora was the killer, Lexy was still convinced something was going on at the *K9 Center*. She just didn't know *what* and she didn't want to admit she'd been snooping around behind the building.

Another engine started up.

"That's the last of our cars," Norman said. "We'd better hurry. She'll be starting this place on fire next."

"There's nothing going on at the *K9 Center*." Olivia's hands had been freed and she scooped Farfel up in her arms while Norman worked on the ropes around her legs. "If you must know, Steve and I are working on a special dog food formula. One with special herbs to enhance the dogs' performance in agility."

Lexy undid the last knot around her ankle and looked up at Olivia. "A special dog food formula? That's what all the secrecy was about?"

"Yes. The dog food market is very competitive and if someone discovered our recipe, they might beat us to market and all our hard work would be for nothing."

"So you were researching the herbs and baking the food at the *K9 Center*?"

"That's right," Olivia said. "Steve and I are partners. In fact, we've just perfected the recipe

220

and had some sample bags made, which we were handing off to our potential investor tonight."

Lexy remembered the conversation she'd heard when she was hiding behind the dumpster. "Is your investor named Michael?"

"Yes, how did you know?"

"Oh, just something I heard." Lexy felt silly. She'd imagined a big drug smuggling operation when the whole time all the secrecy had been about dog food. "Anyway, enough chatter. We need to get out of here."

Lexy jumped up from her chair, went to the door and tried pushing, then pulling. The door didn't move even an inch. "It won't budge!"

Sprinkles barked, then clawed at the door. Farfel joined her. The dogs didn't make any more progress than Lexy.

"It's bolted from the outside." Norman tilted his head and closed his eyes. "If I remember correctly, there is a big cast iron bolt that slides down to latch the door shut. It won't slide open unless that bolt is released."

"We'll have to find another way out." Lexy searched the room with frantic eyes. Sprinkles whined at her feet, picking up on Lexy's distress.

"I think the only way out is that window." Olivia pointed to the thin window on the side of the silo.

"That thing's only about six inches wide. None of us would fit through it," Norman said.

"Maybe we could hang out the window and make a ruckus," Olivia offered.

"Who would see or hear us? We're in the middle of nowhere." Lexy's stomach sank and she collapsed onto a bale of hay. "We're trapped in here with one door that we can't budge, a window we can't fit out of and only some *very* flammable hay and pallets to work with."

"Well, like I said before, this is going to make one hell of a story." Norman sounded enthusiastic and Lexy wished she could feel the same way.

"Yeah, I just hope we get out of here to tell it," Olivia replied.

"We may have to wait and try to brave it through the fire." Lexy chewed her bottom lip. "Cora's screwed up the details before. Maybe she won't set it right and it will burn just enough to make an opening for us to get out without killing us."

Norman shot Lexy a dubious look. "That seems dangerous."

"Do you have a better idea?" Lexy unhooked Sprinkles from her leash. She didn't want it getting hung up on a wayward nail or piece of wood if they had to make a quick escape. Sprinkles and Farfel immediately started chasing each other and rolling around. Lexy watched them play, wishing she could be so carefree. As they jumped from hay bale to hay bale, Lexy realized they were using some of the agility techniques in their play. They were both pretty good.

Olivia followed Lexy's gaze, her face lined with worry. "The least she could have done is to have let our dogs go. There's no need to harm them along with us."

Both dogs suddenly stopped and sniffed the air. A few seconds later the acrid smell of smoke burned Lexy's nostrils.

"Do you guys smell smoke?"

Olivia nodded solemnly.

Sprinkles sat in front of Lexy and let out a whimper, her trusting brown eyes looking up at her master.

Lexy's stomach twisted. She couldn't let anything bad happen to Sprinkles. Her eyes searched the room again, stopping at the small window. Too small for a human, but …

"The dogs can fit out that window. We have to get them out."

Olivia jerked her head in the direction of the window. "It's kind of high, but I think they'd be okay. I bet we could set up the hay bales and pallets to make ramps and use the agility commands to get them to jump."

"It's worth a try." Lexy dragged a hay bale into position and Olivia grabbed a pallet.

Was the smell of smoke getting stronger?

Lexy ignored it and pulled another bale of hay over. Norman pitched in and they worked together, building a makeshift ramp and stairway. By the time they were done, the room was hazy with smoke.

"We don't have much time," Lexy said as they put the last piece in place. Norman stood at the uppermost bale of hay. He set a pallet on its side on top of the bale for the dogs could use as a ramp to the window. He stretched onto his tiptoes to look out the window.

"I can see out. But you're right, there's no one out there to hear or see us." His voice was tinged with disappointment.

On the floor, the dogs were circling with excitement. They knew something was up. Lexy scooped up Sprinkles in a big hug and kissed the top of her head.

"You're a good girl. I hope I'll see you in a few." She heard Olivia murmuring something similar to Farfel and then they both put the dogs down and nodded at each other.

"Sprinkles … ramp," Lexy commanded.

Sprinkles circled around the makeshift ramp, looking at Lexy uncertainly. Olivia gave the same command and got the same look from her dog.

"Go!" The two women said at the same time and pointed to the top of the ramp.

The dogs raced to the top.

"Jump!" Lexy and Olivia commanded.

Farfel sailed out the window.

Sprinkles hesitated, looking back at Lexy through the smoke that was now pouring into the room.

"Go on. Jump!" Grief stabbed Lexy's heart as Sprinkles gave her one last look and then disappeared out the window.

Chapter Twenty-Two

"I don't want Lexy's feelings to be hurt, but I think our surveillance skills are a little better than hers," Nans said from the front seat of Ruth's Oldsmobile as she, Ruth, Ida and Helen headed out of town toward the *Fur Fun K9 Center.*

"Well, we certainly need to find out something about Olivia so we can tie these murders to her." Ruth concentrated on driving, her hands at ten o'clock and two o'clock, her neck stretched to see above the steering wheel. "Lexy's investigation out by the dumpster left a lot of questions and our street informants didn't have anything."

"We have more leeway than she does," Helen agreed. "An old lady can walk right into someplace she not supposed to be and no one gets suspicious."

"Right, and if they question us, we just act flustered and they just think we're senile." Ida's comment elicited a fit of giggles from the other ladies.

"We sure do have a lot of advantages. But do we really need these giant ponchos?" Helen gestured to the oversized black canvas poncho that covered her nearly head to toe.

"Oh, yes," Nans said. "We'll be practically invisible outside in the dark with these things on. And if we go inside, we can take them off, or leave them on. No one will think a thing about old ladies in ponchos."

"True. No one notices us anyway," Ruth added.

"When we get there, Ruth, park at the very end so we can slip out of the car and around to that dumpster area Lexy told us about." Nans pressed her lips together. "I'm sure the answer to what Olivia and Steve are up to is out there."

"If that doesn't work, we'll go inside and pretend like we got lost," Helen said. "We can split up and cover more ground that way."

"If we get discovered, we'll just do the usual—act all flustered like we lost our way and ask a lot of questions—then no one will suspect what we are up to," Ida added.

Nans smiled as she looked out the window at the passing farmland. Being an old lady certainly did have its advantages, especially when it came to investigating. It never ceased to amaze her that she could get people to tell her the most incriminating facts by putting on her 'little old lady' act.

The passing scenery lulled her into a trance … and then she jerked awake as she saw a streak of white heading toward the car from the left.

"Look out!"

Ruth stomped on the brakes, swerving to the right. "What the heck was that?"

Nans rolled down her window, sticking her head out and looking back down the road. "Stop the car, I think that's Sprinkles!"

"Lexy's dog? What would she be doing running loose out here?" Ruth stopped, then backed up slowly.

It *was* Sprinkles ... and she was with a small orange dog.

Nans jumped out. "Sprinkles?"

Sprinkles limped over to Nans, who bent down, allowing the dog to cover her with kisses.

"Looks like she's injured." Helen leapt out of the back of the car and squatted next to the dogs. She lifted Sprinkles front paw, then pressed here and there, causing a tiny yelp from the little white dog. "I don't see any blood, but something happened to her leg."

Nans' blood turned cold as she looked around her.

Where was Lexy?

"Something's wrong," Nans said. "Lexy would never let Sprinkles run around off her leash like this."

The dogs ran two feet toward the house, then back to Nans and Helen, barking anxiously.

"I think they're trying to tell us something," Helen glanced in the direction the dogs had headed. "They want to lead us toward the barn."

Nans followed Helen's gaze. She could see the barn in the distance. Then she squinted, her heart kicking. "Is that smoke?"

The dogs took off toward the barn and Nans didn't have to think twice. Sprinkles *was* trying to tell her something—Lexy was in the barn and she needed help.

"Get in the car, Helen," Nans yelled as she headed for the car. "I think Lexy is in trouble!"

Helen was barely in when Ruth gunned it and the car raced toward the barn. Nans pulled her cell phone out and called Jack.

"Jack, I'm at the old farmhouse on Meadow Road," Nans grabbed onto the armrest as Ruth ran over a hole in the dirt driveway bouncing the car almost into the air. "Sprinkles is running around loose here. Do you know where Lexy is?"

"As far as I know, she's supposed to be at agility … with Sprinkles." Jack's voice was guarded.

"I'm afraid something's wrong. I think I see smoke coming out of the barn next to the old farmhouse," Nans hoped Jack couldn't hear the fear in her voice.

"I'll put in a call. Don't do anything until I get there."

"But Lexy might need us."

"Mona, I'm serious. This could be dangerous. I need you to stand down. Stay in the car and wait for me," Jack ordered, then disconnected before Nans could argue further.

Nans turned in her seat as Ruth pulled up to the barn. The three other ladies looked at her, expectantly.

"What did Jack say?" Ruth cut the engine.

"He said he was coming and he'd call the fire department. We're supposed to wait in the car until he gets here," Nans said fumbling for the seatbelt.

Ida's forehead crumpled into a series of wrinkles. "Are you kidding? Lexy could be in there in trouble … we're not really going to sit in the car, are we?"

The four ladies stared at each other. The only sound in the car was the metallic click of seat belts being unlatched.

"Heck, no!" they yelled at once, shoving their doors open and bursting out of the car.

***

Smoke streamed out of the open barn door. Orange flames licked the right side of the barn … still far enough away from the door to allow them to get inside. Nans covered her mouth with part of her poncho and gestured to Ruth, Ida and Helen to do the same.

The two dogs ran inside the barn, barking and leaping. Nans and the ladies followed.

Inside, it was almost impossible to see. Nans' eyes watered, her lungs burned, but thoughts of Lexy needing her help drove her forward.

"I don't see her!" Ida shouted.

"Over there!" Helen pointed to the right. Sprinkles and the other dog were clawing and whining at a large wooden door that had been bolted shut with an iron bolt. It was in the back of the barn and Nans remembered seeing a small silo sticking up toward the back.

Could Lexy be locked inside the silo?

Nans rushed to the door. Grabbing metal lock, she heaved with all her might, sliding it and unlocking the door. They pushed the door open and they rushed into the smoke-filled room.

Inside, Nans could make out the hazy form of bales of hay stacked up to the window. She could hear the crackling of the building as it heated up. The dogs' barking added to the level of sound. Then she heard Lexy's voice.

"Sprinkles!"

"Lexy?" Nans darted her eyes around the room.

Lexy's trim figure appeared out of the haze. "Nans!"

Nans pulled her close for a hug.

"What are you guys doing here?" Norman had appeared on Nans' right and she hugged him, too.

"Enough with the hugging. The fire is closing in and we better get out of here!" Ida yelled, pointing to the door where orange flames flicked at the right side.

Nans realized Ida was right. They better skedaddle. She pushed Lexy toward the door and was turning in that direction herself when she realized a third person had been in the silo with Lexy and Norman.

As the figure came closer, Nans heart kicked.

It was the killer … Olivia!

And she was coming after Lexy!

"Look out!" Nans yelled.

She pushed Lexy to the side and launched herself at Olivia.

***

Lexy stumbled from Nans' shove, almost falling to the floor. She turned in time to see Nans tackle Olivia with her shoulder. The two women fell to the floor.

"What the heck?"

She turned to Ruth, Ida and Helen who were standing in the doorway of the silo, staring at Nans and Olivia as they wrestled with each other.

"She's got the killer!" Ruth yelled.

That's when Lexy realized Nans didn't know Olivia had also been a victim, trapped in there with them.

"Nans, no! Olivia isn't the killer!" Lexy rushed back toward the two women, trying to pull Nans off Olivia. The smoke was getting thicker on the floor making it difficult to tell who was who. Lexy reached into the pile, grabbed an arm and pulled.

"She isn't?" Ruth, Ida and Helen asked wide eyed.

"No—it was Cora the whole time!" Norman said and they all rushed back to help Lexy pull the two women apart.

"Mona—stop!" Ida grabbed Nans by the belt of her poncho and hauled her up to a standing position.

"I caught her!" Nans pointed at Olivia proudly.

"She's not the killer. Cora is!" Lexy yelled. Farfel ran happy circles around Olivia who pushed herself up from the floor.

Nans gave Olivia a dubious look. "But the evidence …"

"There's no time for that now," Lexy yelled. "We'll explain later!"

They all turned toward the door and Lexy's stomach dropped like a lead sinker. The flames had worked their way all around the door frame.

"We better make a run for it," Nans yelled.

They rushed toward the door.

Crunch!

Lexy stopped short just as the doorway collapsed into a fiery mass of boards.

"Oh. Poo." Helen said.

The exit was almost entirely blocked. There was just a three foot opening, but it was full of flames.

They were trapped.

***

"The ponchos—they're flame retardant!" Nans yelled.

The ladies whipped off their ponchos and started beating the flames back.

Ruth and Helen laid theirs over the tops of the beams that had fallen and the flames snuffed out enough so that they could step over them and out into the barn. Lexy pushed the older women out first, then she, Norman and Olivia followed.

The seven of them burst out of the barn like bees rushing out of a flaming hive.

Lexy turned to look at the burning barn just in time to see Sprinkles sprint out of the doorway. Her eyes filled with tears as she fell to her knees, hugging the small dog.

The rest of them stood bent over with their hands on their knees, sucking in the clean air as the sound of sirens drew closer.

"Wait … where's Farfel?" Olivia's voice rose in panic as she whirled around looking for the small dog. "Farfel!"

A faint yip sounded from inside the barn.

"She's still inside!" Olivia turned, taking a step toward the barn but Norman's hand fell on her shoulder before she could continue.

"No, it's too dangerous," he said.

She struggled to get away from his grasp. "I have to get my baby!"

"I'll go." Norman pushed Olivia to the side and ran toward the barn.

"Norman—wait!" Lexy yelled after him.

But it was too late. Her heart crowded her throat as she watched him disappear into the barn, just as the police and fire trucked pulled onto the lawn beside them.

Jack leapt out of his car rushing to Lexy. "Are you okay?"

"Yes. But Norman ran back there!" Lexy pointed to the barn now almost fully engulfed in flames.

"Someone is in there?" One of the firemen looked up from his task of unrolling the hose.

Lexy nodded.

His mouth twisted into a grim line. "I don't know if there's much of a chance, but we'll send someone in."

Beside her, Olivia wrung her hands and whimpered. Nans, Ruth, Ida and Helen fended off the ministrations of the EMT's, craning their necks, looking toward the barn for any sight of Norman.

"Look! Over there!" Ruth pointed to the furthest edge of the barn. The landscape dipped downhill, exposing the cellar. A figure covered in soot wriggled out from the window.

Lexy's heart swelled when she recognized the figure. "It's Norman and he's got Farfel!"

Olivia broke into a sprint, running toward them and grabbing Farfel from Norman, then showering the dog with kisses. Nans, Ruth, Ida and Helen surrounded Norman, patting him on the back. Lexy could see a blush creeping onto his soot-streaked cheeks.

"What happened?" Jack asked.

With Norman running back into the fire, Lexy had forgotten all about Cora. She whirled around to answer Jack. "Cora's getting away! You have to hurry!" she said with breathless urgency.

"Whoa," Jack put his hands on Lexy's shoulders. "Slow down. Take a deep breath and tell me what you are talking about."

Lexy took a deep breath and told him how Cora was the granddaughter of the farmer who owned the land before Regis' company bought it and how she'd locked them in the silo and set it on fire.

"She's the one who killed Winston and Regis out of revenge for the way they practically stole the land from her grandfather," she finished.

"Do you know her last name?"

Lexy nodded. "Silversteen."

"Don't move." Jack brushed his lips across her forehead, then ran back to the police car.

The yard was a hive of activity. Two ambulances were parked and EMT's were looking over Nans and the other ladies. Firefighters rushed around, aiming hoses gushing loudly with water at the barn fire.

Lexy walked over to Nans, Ruth, Ida, Helen, Norman and Olivia who were in a cluster ten feet away. Surely Jack didn't mean she couldn't walk ten feet?

"Are you okay?" she asked Norman, who was being tended to by an EMT.

"Yep," he grinned. That little dog showed me a trapdoor in the main barn and we got out through the basement. He reached out to pet Farfel's singed fur.

Sprinkles barked and Lexy bent down to pet her, then turned to Nans. "How did you guys know we were in there?"

Nans smiled down at Sprinkles. "Actually, it was Sprinkles that told us."

"Huh?"

"We were driving down the road and saw her running around loose," Nans said. "We knew you'd never let her loose so we called Jack, then came to investigate."

"Well, thanks. And thanks to you, too, Sprinkles." Lexy kissed the top of the dog's head then stood and hugged Nans.

"You saved our lives." Lexy turned to face Ruth, Ida and Helen. "All of you."

"Gosh, it was nothing, Lexy," Ruth stammered.

"But, what *were* you doing driving down this road?" Lexy's brows dipped as she studied the 'deer-in-the-headlights' looks on the ladies faces.

What had they been up to?

She never got her answer because just then Jack joined them, his phone up to his ear. "They're putting out an A.P.B. for Cora. Are you sure no one else was inside?"

Lexy nodded. "It was just us three in the silo and then Nans and the ladies came to our rescue. Everyone is out."

"Call Mike and tell him not to come," Jack barked into the phone. "Thankfully we won't need a medical examiner here today."

"You can say that again," Nans said.

"Yes. Thank goodness everyone survived," Ruth echoed.

"Oh, that, too. But that's not exactly what I meant." Nans shot them a sheepish look. "I was glad he wasn't coming because I haven't had a chance to bake him that apple pie yet."

Chapter Twenty-Three

"Look at this—a page one article with my by-line and everything!" Norman held up the front page of the Brook Ridge Tribune, his face alive with excitement.

It was the day after the fire and they'd gathered in the front room of Lexy's bakery—Norman, Lexy, Jack, Anna, Nans and the three ladies. Even Olivia, Larry and Evelyn had joined them. Lexy had put out a tray of pastries and the aromatic smell of rich coffee filled the room.

"That's wonderful, Norman," Nans said.

"I'm just glad the headline doesn't read 'Killer Caterer Murders Millionaire'," Anna joked.

"Me, too," Lexy said. "That could have really killed our businesses."

Anna laughed. "Yep, but I knew *we* didn't make the mistake and that you and Nans would figure it all out in the end."

"And, hopefully this is the first of many front page articles." Norman nodded to Nans, Ruth, Ida and Helen in turn. "As well as the beginning of collaborating on many cases together."

"Here, here!" The four ladies raised champagne glasses filled with thick green juice and clinked them against Norman's glass.

"And don't forget that *you* were the hero of the day," Olivia gushed, referring to Norman's heroic rescue of Farfel from the clutches of the fire.

A blush crept up Norman's neck. "Yeah, I guess I did finally do something heroic and it's great that both dogs have a clean bill of health."

"Don't go getting too big for your britches." Ida wagged a finger at him. "You still owe us a cleanup after coffee. And you too, Lexy."

Lexy grimaced. "That's right. Too bad our cars are at the bottom of the pond. It might be a while before I can get over to Nans'."

"They did pull the cars out of the pond, actually," Jack said. "But I don't think you guys are going to want them back. That pond has a very muddy bottom and your cars are full of it. I hope you had good insurance."

"Well, at least you caught Cora," Olivia said.

"Yep, we got her at the airport right before she headed off on a one-way trip to Mexico." Jack reached into his back pocket and pulled out an envelope. "We found Wolf's computer and the folder with the photographs of the birthday party in her apartment. They're still at the police station as evidence, but we took the liberty of printing out the pictures for you."

Olivia slowly took the envelope Jack was holding out toward her. She flipped open the flap and thumbed through the pictures inside.

"These are the pictures from the birthday party. The last pictures of Daddy." She sniffed as her eyes filled with tears.

Larry put his arm around her, glancing in at the pictures. "It's great that we've got these of Daddy and Winston, too. I'm sorry they're gone, but we still have each other."

Olivia beamed up at him.

"Well, Larry, I'll admit this juice is tasty." Nans took a sip from her glass, then puckered her lips. "But I have to say I prefer coffee."

Larry chuckled. "I wanted to bring you some seeing as the juice almost made me a murder suspect."

Nans blanched. "Well, it *did* seem like the perfect way to poison him."

Larry shrugged. "I always brought fresh juice to the club on Wednesdays, trying to get people on the health band wagon … and drum up business for the market. So, naturally I brought some that day for Winston to drink."

Nans nodded. "What were you two arguing about that day?"

243

Larry's face fell. "After I talked to you about him at the Farmer's Market, it got me thinking that maybe I should try to help him with his gambling and anger problems. But, he wouldn't even admit he had them. It got kind of heated and we argued."

"Now, that's not your fault." Evelyn patted Larry's arm.

"Right, let's look on the positive side." Larry put his hand over Evelyn's. "The three of us get to control the company now and we can put the corporate resources to good use."

"That's right," Evelyn nodded. "We can stop the retail development of that beautiful land on Meadow Road and use it for a community organic farming initiative instead."

"And branch out into the herbal dog food business." Larry winked at Olivia.

Olivia's smile widened. "And now that Steve and I will have corporate backing for the dog food line, we can start production right away instead of waiting for an investor. And get a proper facility instead of fiddling around in secret in the back rooms of the *K9 Center*."

"We're going to be able to do a lot of good with that company now. Change the way it operates and instill a new company culture and traditions," Evelyn said.

"And start new family traditions, too," Larry added giving both Olivia and Evelyn a hug.

Lexy's heart surged for the three of them. It looked like this whole nasty business had a silver lining after all. Olivia and Larry were going to get the close relationship they both had said they missed and Larry and Evelyn were free to become more than just in-laws.

"Looks like all's well that ends well." Ida summed up Lexy's feelings as she bit into her lemon square.

"Except for the part where I have to go on a date with Stan," Helen said. Everyone laughed. Lexy had almost forgotten about the big sacrifice Helen had made for the sake of getting information on the case.

Jack slid his arm around Lexy's shoulders. "I hope you ladies have had enough sleuthing for a while. Especially you, Lexy."

Lexy chewed on her bottom lip, eyeing Nans and the other women's expectant faces. She knew none of them would want to take a break from sleuthing, but the truth was she *could* use a little less excitement in her life for the moment.

"Well, I *do* need to focus on the bakery," she said. "I've been neglecting it while chasing leads on this case, so some down time might not be a bad thing."

Nans, Ruth, Ida and Helen nodded.

"We wouldn't want to run out of pastries to bribe our suspects with," Ruth joked.

"And don't forget, we have a lot of work to do packing up my house," Jack reminded her. "In fact, I'd like to claim your spare time for the rest of the summer."

Lexy smiled up at Jack. Giving him all her spare time didn't seem like such a bad idea at all. Of course, she could think of much more interesting things they could be doing than boxing up old dishes, but maybe they could fit some of those interesting things in in-between packing and cleaning.

Yep, now that she thought about it, taking a break from sleuthing to get Jack's house ready for sale didn't seem like such a bad idea at all.

After all, what trouble could she possibly get into while cleaning decades of clutter out of an old house?

The end.

Lemon Squares Recipe

Lemon Squares Recipe

I found this recipe tucked inside one of my mom's old recipe books from the 1960s. It was handwritten on a thin, yellowed piece of paper and dotted with stains (probably lemon juice). She made the best lemon squares—I hope you enjoy them as much as I used to when I was a kid!

For the crust:

1 cup flour
1/4 cup confectioner's sugar
1/2 cup butter or margarine

Blend the above ingredients and press into a 9x9 pan. Bake at 350 (f) for 20 minutes.
While baking, mix the following together for the topping:

1 cup sugar
2 eggs
2 tablespoons lemon juice
1/2 teaspoon baking powder
1 1/2 teaspoon flour

Pour the mixture over the top of the baked crust layer. Bake at 350 (f) for 25 minutes, cool and cut into bars.

Note: you can reserve some of the crust mixture and sprinkle it over the top of the filling.

If you want more bars, double the ingredients and cook in a 13x9 pan.

Snickerdoodles Recipe

This is another recipe from my mom's collection. She used to use Crisco like it was going out of style, so that's what she would have used for the shortening ingredient. You can substitute butter for that if you want.

Ingredients:

1 cup shortening, softened
1 1/2 cups sugar
2 eggs
2 3/4 cup flour
2 teaspoons cream of tartar
1 teaspoon baking soda
1/2 teaspoon salt
2 tablespoons sugar
2 teaspoons cinnamon

Procedure:

Preheat oven to 400 degrees (F).

Mix the shortening (or butter), sugar and eggs together thoroughly.

Sift the flour, cream of tartar, baking soda and salt together and then stir into the shortening mixture. Mix thoroughly.

Roll the dough into teaspoon sized balls. Roll each ball in the sugar and cinnamon.

Place balls two inches apart on ungreased cookie sheets.

Bake for about 8 minutes.

A Note From The Author

Thanks so much for reading my cozy mystery "*Ice Cream Murder*". I hope you liked reading it as much as I loved writing it. If you did, and feel inclined to leave a review, I really would appreciate it.

This is book nine of the Lexy Baker series. You can find the rest of the books on my website *http://www.leighanndobbs.com*.

Also, if you like cozy mysteries, you might like my book "*Dead Wrong*" which is book one in the Blackmoore Sisters series. Set in the seaside town of Noquitt Maine, the Blackmoore sisters will take you on a journey of secrets, romance and maybe even a little magic. I have an excerpt from it at the end of this book.

This book has been through many edits with several people and even some software programs, but since nothing is infallible (even the software programs) you might catch a spelling error or mistake and, if you do, I sure would appreciate it if you let me know - you can contact me at *lee@leighanndobbs.com*.

I love to connect with my readers so please do visit me on Facebook at *http://www.facebook.com/leighanndobbsbooks*

Signup to get my newest releases at a discount and notification of contests:
http://www.leighanndobbs.com/newsletter

About The Author

Leighann Dobbs discovered her passion for writing after a twenty year career as a software engineer. She lives in New Hampshire with her husband Bruce, their trusty Chihuahua mix Mojo and beautiful rescue cat, Kitty. When she's not reading, gardening or selling antiques, she likes to write romance and cozy mystery novels and novelettes which are perfect for the busy person on the go.

Find out about her latest books and how to get discounts on them by signing up at:

http://www.leighanndobbs.com/newsletter

Connect with Leighann on Facebook and Twitter

http://facebook.com/leighanndobbsbooks
http://twitter.com/leighanndobbs

***

More Books By Leighann Dobbs

Lexy Baker
Cozy Mystery Series
* * *

Lexy Baker Cozy Mystery Series Boxed Set Vol 1
(Books 1-4)

Or buy the books separately:

Killer Cupcakes (Book 1)
Dying For Danish (Book 2)
Murder, Money and Marzipan (Book 3)
3 Bodies and a Biscotti (Book 4)
Brownies, Bodies & Bad Guys (Book 5)
Bake, Battle & Roll (Book 6)
Wedded Blintz (Book 7)
Scones, Skulls & Scams (Book 8)
Ice Cream Murder (Book 9)

Mystic Notch
Cats & Magic Cozy Mystery Series
* * *

Ghostly Paws

Blackmoore Sisters
Cozy Mystery Series
* * *

Dead Wrong
Dead & Buried
Dead Tide
Buried Secrets

Kate Diamond
Adventure/Suspense Series
* * *

Hidden Agemda

Contemporary
Romance
* * *

Sweet Escapes
Reluctant Romance

Dobbs "Fancytales"
Regency Romance Fairytales Series
* * *

Something In Red
Snow White and the Seven Rogues
Dancing On Glass
The Beast of Edenmaine
The Reluctant Princess

Excerpt From Dead Wrong:

Morgan Blackmoore tapped her finger lightly on the counter, her mind barely registering the low buzz of voices behind her in the crowded coffee shop as she mentally prioritized the tasks that awaited her back at her own store.

"Here you go, one yerba mate tea and a vanilla latte." Felicity rang up the purchase, as Morgan dug in the front pocket of her faded denim jeans for some cash which she traded for the two paper cups.

Inhaling the spicy aroma of the tea, she turned to leave, her long, silky black hair swinging behind her. Elbowing her way through the crowd, she headed toward the door. At this time of morning, the coffee shop was filled with locals and Morgan knew almost all of them well enough to exchange a quick greeting or nod.

Suddenly a short, stout figure appeared, blocking her path. Morgan let out a sharp breath, recognizing the figure as Prudence Littlefield.

Prudence had a long running feud with the Blackmoores which dated back to some sort of run-in she'd had with Morgan's grandmother when they were young girls. As a result, Prudence loved to harass and berate the Blackmoore girls in public. Morgan's eyes darted around the room, looking for an escape route.

"Just who do you think you are?" Prudence demanded, her hands fisted on her hips, legs spaced shoulder width apart. Morgan noticed she was wearing her usual knee high rubber boots and an orange sunflower scarf.

Morgan's brow furrowed over her ice blue eyes as she stared at the older woman's prune like face.

"Excuse me?"

"Don't you play dumb with me Morgan Blackmoore. What kind of concoction did you give my Ed? He's been acting plumb crazy."

Morgan thought back over the previous week's customers. Ed Littlefield *had* come into her herbal remedies shop, but she'd be damned if she'd announce to the whole town what he was after.

She narrowed her eyes at Prudence. "That's between me and Ed."

Prudence's cheeks turned crimson. Her nostrils flared. "You know what *I* think," she said narrowing her eyes and leaning in toward Morgan, "I think you're a witch, just like your great-great-great-grandmother!"

Morgan felt an angry heat course through her veins. There was nothing she hated more than being called a witch. She was a Doctor of Pharmacology with a Master Herbalist's license, not some sort of spell-casting conjurer.

The coffee shop had grown silent. Morgan could feel the crowd staring at her. She leaned forward, looking wrinkled old Prudence Littlefield straight in the eye.

"Well now, I think we know that's not true," she said, her voice barely above a whisper, "Because if I was a witch, I'd have turned you into a newt long ago."

Then she pushed her way past the old crone and fled out the coffee shop door.

***

Fiona Blackmoore stared at the amethyst crystal in front of her wondering how to work it into a pendant. On most days, she could easily figure out exactly how to cut and position the stone, but right now her brain was in a pre-caffeine fog.

Where was Morgan with her latte?

She sighed, looking at her watch. It was ten past eight, Morgan should be here by now, she thought impatiently.

Fiona looked around the small shop, *Sticks and Stones*, she shared with her sister. An old cottage that had been in the family for generations, it sat at one of the highest points in their town of Noquitt, Maine.

Turning in her chair, she looked out the back window. In between the tree trunks that made up a small patch of woods, she had a bird's eye view of the sparkling, sapphire blue Atlantic Ocean in the distance.

The cottage sat about 500 feet inland at the top of a high cliff that plunged into the Atlantic. If the woods were cleared, like the developers wanted, the view would be even better. But Fiona would have none of that, no matter how much the developers offered them, or how much they needed the money. She and her sisters would never sell the cottage.

She turned away from the window and surveyed the inside of the shop. One side was setup as an apothecary of sorts. Antique slotted shelves loaded with various herbs lined the walls. Dried weeds hung from the rafters and several mortar and pestles stood on the counter, ready for whatever herbal concoctions her sister was hired to make.

On her side sat a variety of gemologist tools and a large assortment of   crystals. Three antique oak and glass jewelry cases displayed her creations. Fiona smiled as she looked at them. Since childhood she had been fascinated with rocks and gems so it was no surprise to anyone when she grew up to become a gemologist and jewelry designer, creating jewelry not only for its beauty, but also for its healing properties.

The two sisters vocations suited each other perfectly and they often worked together providing customers with crystal and herbal healing for whatever ailed them.

The jangling of the bell over the door brought her attention to the front of the shop. She breathed a sigh of relief when Morgan burst through the door, her cheeks flushed, holding two steaming paper cups.

"What's the matter?" Fiona held her hand out, accepting the drink gratefully. Peeling back the plastic tab, she inhaled the sweet vanilla scent of the latte.

"I just had a run in with Prudence Littlefield!" Morgan's eyes flashed with anger.

"Oh? I saw her walking down Shore road this morning wearing that god-awful orange sunflower scarf. What was the run-in about this time?" Fiona took the first sip of her latte, closing her eyes and waiting for the caffeine to power her blood stream. She'd had her own run-ins with Pru Littlefield and had learned to take them in stride.

"She was upset about an herbal mix I made for Ed. She called me a witch!"

"What did you make for him?"

"Just some Ginkgo, Ginseng and Horny Goat Weed … although the latter he said was for Prudence."

Fiona's eyes grew wide. "Aren't those herbs for impotence?"

Morgan shrugged "Well, that's what he wanted."

"No wonder Prudence was mad…although you'd think just being married to her would have caused the impotence."

Morgan burst out laughing. "No kidding. I had to question his sanity when he asked me for it. I thought maybe he had a girlfriend on the side."

Fiona shook her head trying to clear the unwanted images of Ed and Prudence Littlefield together.

"Well, I wouldn't let it ruin my day. You know how *she* is."

Morgan put her tea on the counter, then turned to her apothecary shelf and picked several herbs out of the slots. "I know, but she always seems to know how to push my buttons. Especially when she calls me a witch."

Fiona grimaced. "Right, well I wish we *were* witches. Then we could just conjure up some money and not be scrambling to pay the taxes on this shop and the house."

Morgan sat in a tall chair behind the counter and proceeded to measure dried herbs into a mortar.

"I know. I saw Eli Stark in town yesterday and he was pestering me about selling the shop again."

"What did you tell him?"

"I told him we'd sell over our dead bodies." Morgan picked up a pestle and started grinding away at the herbs.

Fiona smiled. Eli Stark had been after them for almost a year to sell the small piece of land their shop sat on. He had visions of buying it, along with some adjacent lots in order to develop the area into high end condos.

Even though their parents early deaths had left Fiona, Morgan and their two other sisters property rich but cash poor the four of them agreed they would never sell. Both the small shop and the stately ocean home they lived in had been in the family for generations and they didn't want *their* generation to be the one that lost them.

The only problem was, although they owned the properties outright, the taxes were astronomical and, on their meager earnings, they were all just scraping by to make ends meet.

All the more reason to get this necklace finished so I can get paid. Thankfully, the caffeine had finally cleared the cobwebs in her head and Fiona was ready to get to work. Staring down at the amethyst, a vision of the perfect shape to cut the stone appeared in her mind. She grabbed her tools and started shaping the stone.

Fiona and Morgan were both lost in their work. They worked silently, the only sounds in the little shop being the scrape of mortar on pestle and the hum of Fiona's gem grinding tool mixed with a few melodic tweets and chirps that floated in from the open window.

Fiona didn't know how long they were working like that when the bell over the shop door chimed again. She figured it must have been an hour or two judging by the fact that the few sips left in the bottom of her latte cup had grown cold.

She smiled, looking up from her work to greet their potential customer, but the smile froze on her face when she saw who it was.

Sheriff Overton stood in the door flanked by two police officers. A toothpick jutted out of the side of Overton's mouth and judging by the looks on all three of their faces, they weren't there to buy herbs or crystals.

Fiona could almost hear her heart beating in the silence as the men stood there, adjusting their eyes to the light and getting their bearings.

"Can we help you?" Morgan asked, stopping her work to wipe her hands on a towel.

Overton's head swiveled in her direction like a hawk spying a rabbit in a field.

"That's her." He nodded to the two uniformed men who approached Morgan hesitantly. Fiona recognized one of the men as Brody Hunter, whose older brother Morgan had dated all through high school. She saw Brody look questioningly at the Sheriff.

The other man stood a head taller than Brody. Fiona noticed his dark hair and broad shoulders but her assessment of him stopped there when she saw him pulling out a pair of handcuffs.

Her heart lurched at the look of panic on her sister's face as the men advanced toward her.

"Just what is this all about?" She demanded, standing up and taking a step toward the Sheriff.

There was no love lost between the Sheriff and Fiona. They'd had a few run-ins and she thought he was an egotistical bore and probably crooked too. He ignored her question focusing his attention on Morgan. The next words out of his mouth chilled Fiona to the core.

"Morgan Blackmoore … you're under arrest for the murder of Prudence Littlefield."

Made in United States
Orlando, FL
04 June 2023

33819037R00147